# JOY COWLEY

was born at Levin in 1936. Among her published works are five adult novels, three junior novels (two of which won the book of the year award), several children's picture books, more than 400 children's reading books which are used worldwide, two books of reflections, and many short stories and articles. She is now married to Terry Coles and lives in the Marlborough Sounds. Joy was awarded the New Zealand Commemoration Medal in 1990 and the OBE in 1992, for services to children's literature.

JOY COWLEY

# THE COMPLETE SHORT STORIES

Flamingo
*An Imprint of* HarperCollins*Publishers*

Flamingo
An imprint of HarperCollinsPublishers

First published 1997
HarperCollinsPublishers New Zealand Limited
P.O. Box 1, Auckland

ISBN 1 86950 250 7

Cover by Dexter Fry
Designed and typeset by Dexter Fry
Printed by Wright and Carman (NZ) Ltd, Wellington

# Joy Cowley

## The Complete Short Stories

# ACKNOWLEDGMENTS

'Heart Attack', 'Going to the Mountain', 'All About Love', 'Flowers' and 'The Cleaning of Windows' are previously unpublished. The other stories in this volume were originally published as follows: 'The Kite' — *NZ Listener*, November 1963; 'The Moth' — *Landfall*, September 1964; 'The Silk', *NZ Listener*, March 1965; 'House with a View' — *NZ Listener*, October 1965; 'The Woman Next Door' — *NZ Listener*, September 1967, originally entitled 'A Place to Go'; 'Rural Delivery' — *NZ Listener*, June 1976; 'God Loves You, Miss Rosewater' — *NZ Listener*, March 1978; 'The Colonel and South America' — *Islands*, August 1978; 'Apple Wine' — *Islands*, June 1980; 'Distances' — *The Tablet*, March 1983; 'The Machinery of Dreams' — The Summer Book 2, Port Nicholson Press, 1983; 'Journey' — *NZ Listener*, July 1988.

# CONTENTS

In memory of Malcolm Mason,
a truly great man who wore his
greatness as though he had bought
it in a second-hand shop.

# PROLOGUE

Before the beginning there was another beginning, and another beginning before that, so although I could say that it all began with *The New Zealand Listener*, it would be more correct to say I've been story-making all my life. Children are very versatile in the ways they manage their lives. Their imaginations will readily tackle the unexplained and unexplainable and without effort they can take the fiction of living and convert it to the truth of myth. So, there were always stories, long serials told to my sisters each night, swashbuckling heroines who disguised themselves as boys so they could have adventures. Adventure was the key word. It was linked to noble deeds and exciting countries (New Zealand didn't rate a place in the imagination in those days) but even then, when all that I recognised was a delight in story-telling, the story was a way of spending excess emotional energy, a way of deflecting pain.

In adolescence the stories became introspective, self-indulgent in their melancholy: tales of adventure gave way to the tragedy of grand opera. Like others of my age, I was graduating from a world of action to a world of feeling. I have noticed that this kind of melancholy fiction is typical of the emerging writer, regardless of age.

For me, the *Listener* marks the most significant beginning. In 1960, pregnant for the fourth time in as many years, I saw the last of my great adventure tales fading into the sunset — I gave up the dream of becoming a painter and decided to try selling stories. My ambition was to have a short story published in the *Listener*.

Support has always been important. Writing is a form of communication, a way of loving, and it always has to be for someone. I was surrounded by people who generously gifted their time and patience, who read stories and offered helpful advice. The Manawatu Writers' Group became an extension of family. I was parasitic in my hunger for affirmation.

During 1960 and 1961 I sent stories to the *Listener* at the rate of two or three a month and they all came back, not with rejection slips but with positively worded letters from the man who has most influenced my writing, M.H. Holcroft. As editor of *The New Zealand Listener*, Monte Holcroft deliberately fostered New Zealand literature during the Fifties and Sixties, and most writers of my generation are in his debt. Whatever I have written since, has contained my gratitude.

These days, storymaking flows out into several areas: novels, children's books and stories and plays; educational material, spiritual reflection, short stories, the occasional bout of bad verse. Much of what I do is commissioned and tied to formulae, but every story, whether for adults or children, still begins with the heart, something I've mentioned in a light little story called 'All About Love'. The story which comes head first as an intellectual exercise, will never be born alive: it remains a corpse and decomposes with repeated writings until I end up burying it. But since stories must begin with the heart, the intellect can know little about them until the work is finished. Then the mind reads them, as it were, for the first time. This means that only when a story is down on paper, can I be intelligent about it and say, 'Ah yes, this is what I did, and this and that.' Only then can I see how some stimulus has set the heart in motion, that heart of being which is cosmic and eternal and at one with everything else. I see then how I have taken dictation word by word. And I have been many times shaken by the way stories can accurately predict the future.

The only story which had not been prophetic in that way was 'The Silk', written more than twenty years ago. It has been the most influential of all my stories and has appeared in many anthologies. Certainly, for me it had great power in the writing process.

Then, this winter, my husband and I had to live through 'The Silk' together, knowing what was happening and yet helpless within its detail. As Malcolm lay in bed, awaiting death, we looked out through frostcrystals on the window, talked of the past, filled hot water bottles, planned the funeral. I searched for exotic foods to tempt his appetite and resented the twice weekly visits from the district nurse. Malcolm said he wanted to be buried in the brocade dressing gown I had bought him when we were engaged. We took it out of the wardrobe, turned back the lining and saw the label, '100% pure silk'. Then we reread the story together and were struck by parallels too consistent for coincidence. Malcolm remarked that prophecy fell down in the request for a double plot. ('You'll get a double plot, won't you, Amy? I wouldn't rest easy thinking you were going to sleep by someone else.') Cemeteries these days didn't have double plots, he said.

Malcolm died in the night. I woke up, kissed his cheek, discovered that it was cold, and my first thought was, 'He didn't say goodbye!' Later that day, the funeral director asked if we would like a double plot. Oh yes, double plots were still available in the returned servicemen's part of the cemetery.

I know writers who are almost fearful of this clairvoyant element in their writing. I'm sometimes in awe of it, but it doesn't worry me, and it does reinforce my view that the artist is medium rather than creator.

It's a quarter of a century since that conscious decision to try for publication in the *Listener*. I don't know how many stories I have written in that time, but I have chosen this collection because they have in some way satisfied me, because they contain truth. Don't ask me what I mean by truth. But I do know it when I meet it. It belongs to the heart and to eternity, and it is cool to the touch.

The first twelve stories show the journey from youth to middle age. Stories one to five, written in the 1960s, show a certain simplicity. I see them as linear, gauche, fresh, naive. The next seven show more detachment. They are more complex, and have elements of irony. 'Going to the Mountain' is a thinly disguised presentation of marvellous dreams I've had throughout my life — of going to a mountain, of trying to reach a mystical magical snow. 'All About Love' is a game of light and shade in which I make jokes at the writer's expense just in case people, including myself, take me too seriously. And the fourteenth story in the collection is not really a story at all but paintings of events in a year of my youth.

My gratitude to Bert Hingley who insisted that these stories come together, and to Roseleen Yurjevich for making sense of them with her typing skills.

Special thanks to my stepson Andrew Mason who is always available to read and offer helpful suggestions, and who, as a freelance editor, maintains the tradition of fostering New Zealand writing.

The patterns of life are indeed charming.

# THE KITE

O nce upon a windy day there was a man and a boy and a kite with seven tails. The boy was too young to have flown a kite before, the man too old to remember, so that the sensation of being drawn between heaven and earth by a string was new to them both.

It started when the boy ran out to play and found, on the lawn, a tea-towel that the wind had snatched from the next-door clothesline. He wriggled through a gap in the hedge, waving and calling until the old man came out from his house.

After he had handed back the towel, the boy stayed, talking about the wind and looking for the jar of sweets that was usually kept on the window ledge. The old man saw the thought in the boy's eyes but couldn't tell him the jar was empty. Instead, he too talked about the wind.

'Good day for kites,' he said.

'For what?' said the boy, and the old man realised that he had never seen one.

He went back to his kitchen and felt on the mantelpiece for the pension money that he had hidden behind the clock, then he took his coat and stick, told the boy to wait, and shuffled off towards the corner block of shops.

As soon as he had gone, the boy ran through the hedge to tell his mother. He was getting a great big kite thing that flied up on the wind, and could they make it go in the paddock behind the house? His mother looked doubtful but said yes, and the boy went back to wait. He was still there, sitting on the doorstep, when the old man came back with the parcel under his arm.

'Got it,' said the old man. 'I knew they had one there. Saw it in the window last time I went past.'

The parcel was long and round, more like a tube of something or a baseball bat.

'That's all?' said the boy.

'We've got to put it together yet. Here —' The old man put the parcel on the boy's lap and carefully, as though he were on a narrow platform high above the ground, sat down.

'This is the kite,' he said, unwrapping a tube of pink plastic. 'And these wooden bits are the spars that fit in these pockets. And all the other pieces make tails to go on here. I got a ball of string too.'

'You know how to make it?' asked the boy.

'No making in this thing. It's all done for you.' The old man looked up at the sky, far beyond the limit of his vision, then said slowly, 'A long time ago I made a beauty of a kite. I had a boy like you and I made him this kite — paper, it was, and shaped like a big fish. We painted it gold and it had red eyes that kind of shone in the sun. And once the wind got it it'd stay up for hours. Some kites don't fly too good, but this was a real beauty.'

'Have you still got it?' said the boy, who didn't know how long a long time ago was.

'No.' The old man shook his head and went back to fitting the cross pieces.

'What happened to it?'

'I think we lost it.'

'How?'

'Well — I don't remember too clear, but I think the string

2

broke. It got away on us.'

'Where?' asked the boy, leaning closer. 'Did the wind take it?'

'Right up into the middle of the sky.'

'Up to the stars?'

'Oh, way past the stars and on towards the moon. It's probably still there if it hasn't banged into something.' He smiled as he saw, through half-shut eyes, the great goldfish swimming slowly round the bowl of the moon.

'Will my kite fly as high as that?' asked the boy.

'Nearly, it's a big ball of string.' He stooped over the task in front of him but his fingers, stiff as the roots of a tree, refused to obey. 'Can you do knots?' he asked. 'All right, tie these on here. They're the tails and if you don't have them right, the kite won't be balanced properly.'

With his head lowered between the old man's and the kite, the boy fastened six lengths of plastic, then the string, as he was directed. Already the kite was a living thing, anxious for its freedom. It vibrated in the backwash of air currents and moved impatiently against their knees.

'Ready now?' said the boy.

The old man handed him the kite. Then he shut his eyes and held his breath, willing his legs to support him. Slowly he stood up.

'Come on,' said the boy. 'I want to make it fly.'

As he reached for his stick, the old man sighed a curse against his weakness. Then, with the boy beside him, the kite between them, he walked up the path.

Along the path and through the gate they went, to a world of windswept grass; acres and acres of green that rippled round their ankles. The old man stopped to unroll the ball of string.

'You'll have to run it up,' he said.

'Run?' The boy stood swaying with the power of his arms.

'Hold it out to the side and run. When you feel the wind catch it, let go.'

He unwound the string and watched. Released to the air, the

kite was like a mad thing, soaring and diving, dipping sideways then straightening in a flurry of colour. The boy shrieked and clapped his hands, but the old man shook his head.

'Bring it in,' he said. 'We'll try it with another tail.'

They hauled it in and the boy tied on another length of plastic. When he let it go this time, it swooped up with the wind and climbed in a zigzag pattern above their heads, up and up, as high as the string allowed. The old man had the end looped round his hand. He could feel the rhythm of the wind in every muscle of his arm.

'Let me hold it!' the boy shouted.

'Think you can?'

The boy grabbed the string in front of the old man and held it tight in both hands. But he was small, and at the other end the whole sky pulled against him. Eventually he let go, breathless and laughing; and the old man, whose strength was even smaller, felt the cord bite into his fingers.

'I think we'll tie it on to something,' he said.

He went down the hill to a fence that divided the length of the paddock, and fastened the end of the string to a post. Securely tethered, the kite swung above them, every tail fluttering with indignation. The boy ran to and fro, trying to follow its path. His noise tired the old man. The effort of walking, the excitement, tired him. The wind tired him and took his breath away. A great weariness spread through him. He sat down in the grass and leaned against the fence-post and thought of the other kite until it became a real fish in a sea of turbulent blue. Jonah's whale with fierce red eyes. And a boy that laughed as this one.

After a while the boy sat down beside him.

'Did your kite go this high?'

He nodded.

'As good as this one?'

Again, he nodded.

'I bet your boy liked playing with it. Where is he now — your

4

boy like me? He doesn't live with you, does he?'

'No, I lost him in the war.'

'War?' It was one of those adult words that he knew nothing about.

'You mean — lost like the kite?'

Too tired to explain, the old man nodded. 'That's right,' he said. And it was right. The soldier in the photo by his bed was a stranger.

Now there was a boy, young and free as the wind, who chased a paper fish across the heavens.

The boy at his side tugged his sleeve and pointed. 'Look, it's nearly up to the clouds. I bet Mum can see it, I bet she's watching through the kitchen window.'

At that moment, his mother was pegging a shirt on the line. She could see neither the boy nor the old man, but high above the paddocks bobbed the kite. She smiled and went inside to make a cup of tea.

'Can we make it go higher?' asked the boy.

'No more string.'

'I want it to go right up. Like your kite. Up to the moon.'

The old man shook his head. The noise, the wind, the weariness were all too much. They combined and overpowered him.

'I know what!' the boy said. 'We can let it go.'

'No.'

'Yes!'

'No,' he said. 'That's too easy.'

'I want to let it go!' said the boy. 'I want it to bang into the moon. Untie it, cut it with your knife!'

'It's your kite,' said the old man, 'your decision.'

But decision was another of those grown-up words that the boy did not understand. 'Please!' he said.

Please, said the kite, dipping and begging for freedom. The old man turned his head towards it and saw two kites, one pink, one gold, two kites leaping through space like glowing comets.

5

'Give it to me,' he said.

For a moment he held the cord and felt the throb of life as the kite strained away from him. Then he cut it with his knife.

The boy's mother saw the kite go.

'Oh dear, what a shame,' she said to the dishes. She watched it plunge beyond the frame of the window. 'Such a shame,' and she shook her head. Now there was nothing to be seen in the sky but wind. And nothing in the paddock but wind, and the small boy who was running towards the house.

# The Moth

When she went out to answer the phone she left the door ajar and the moth flew in and bumped about the dinner table. At first he barely noticed it, so tight was the circle of thought that he had drawn round himself and the woman in the next room. He looked at the moth without seeing it; nor did he hear it crash against the empty wine bottle. He sat very still, sensing nothing of his surroundings in his search against time for words, the right words, in sentences that would sound convincing.

There must be no apologies, he thought. She would despise me for that. No, a statement, a brief explanation, nothing more. It's quite straightforward when you come to think of it, the only thing that will save us.

But in that, he knew he was thinking of himself, for she was indestructible. He lifted his cup. Admit it, he said to the man in the moon of his coffee. Your concern is not for her. She has nothing to lose, nothing — except you and you can't believe for a moment that you are irreplaceable. You know her better than that.

He put his cup down, carefully, as though he had just seen in it a great and disturbing truth, then he pressed his fingers against his eyes. I don't know her at all, he said. It's a fact. After all these months — nine, nearly ten — I know less than I did the first night I came to this room. His fingertips pushed back the memory. I owe her nothing, he went on. She is demanding and she is careless. She has become a threat to my family. No matter what she says or does, it is finished. I cannot see her again.

For a while he sat in the dark of his own making, listening to the ebb and flow of her voice. He wondered who had phoned her and tried to feel glad that he was now in a position where he did not care.

There can be no other way, he would tell her. It's the only logical solution.

At that moment the moth, which had been spiralling above the candle on the table, went into an aimless dive and hit him on the face. He started back in his chair, wiping the side of his mouth with a gesture of disgust; then he leaned forward to flick the thing off the tablecloth. He did not like moths. Some, he had to admit, were almost attractive in a peculiar way, but there was nothing beautiful about this one. It flopped to the carpet without spreading a wing to break its fall, and lay there vibrating with a sort of intense breathlessness as though waiting for his shoe. He would have killed it but the thought of the shapeless body beneath his foot was intolerable. He shuddered and turned away.

The only logical solution, he began again. But the phrases had dispersed in the interruption and now they swam beneath the shell of his skull, words and fragments of words, capitals and black italics, in the pink mollusc softness. He tried to net them together, sort them out, to press each one in place on the edge of his tongue. It was hopeless. The touch of the moth on his mouth had destroyed the pattern so that now there was nothing but the taste of dust and the panic of knowing that she would be back and that if he let the moment go he could never hope for another.

Involuntarily, his eyes turned back to the carpet, to providence in the guise of an insect.

How will I tell her? What can I say that won't sound ridiculous? Although he only mouthed the words, he imagined that the moth had heard and understood. It began to turn, slowly, clumsily, in a small circle on the floor.

What's that? He leaned across the table to watch. You're spinning. Ah, of course. Go on, spin my little roulette wheel and show me where I go. If you point to the door I make the coward's exit — right now without saying a word. Stop towards my chair and I stay here and play it out. He laughed to think that he had pinned his future through the axis of this idiot creature. Go on, he said. What's it to be?

But the moth did neither of those things. Instead, it widened its circle and left the floor, instinctively climbing back towards the table and the light.

He shook his head at it. I should have known better than to expect help from you. After all, I was going to kill you. He laughed again. What a fine pair we make. You have never had a brain and mine has been drowned in wine. Here we are — a man with an insect half as big as his thumb — one as stupid as the other. I'm afraid there's not much we can do about it.

Without moving his gaze, he put his head on one side to listen to the voice in the room behind him and to the laughter that rippled through the door.

I hate moths, he said to the insect. It had folded itself into a triangle and was now crawling up the candlestick, its fat, pink-ringed body arched and quivering, its legs caressing the black wrought-iron like a miser's fingers.

I have always hated moths, he said. Floppy, crumbling things. No substance. Not real, somehow. The ghosts of decent, sun-loving insects. That's what you are, my friend, a ghost. A mistake of evolution. I loathe you.

But nevertheless, when he realised that the moth had reached the candle and was still crawling upwards, he put out his hand and brushed it back onto the table. No you don't, he said in a different tone. Shame on you, big fellow that you are, for trying such a thing. You should know better. He turned his wineglass upside down and imprisoned the moth on the tablecloth in front of him. I don't suppose you do, he said. Well, let me tell you something. You were on your way to hell, my friend. Fire and brimstone, the broad wax path to destruction. I am your saviour. Do you understand that much?

The moth moved helplessly inside the glass dome, bumping head first into invisible walls and beating its wings so vigorously that a cloud of fine dust filled the wineglass, like a snowstorm round a scene in a paperweight. Every now and then it would try to climb the side, but each time it fell back upside down, its legs waving over its naked body. He watched it, absurdly pleased to have it in his power.

You want to be free, he said. But if I let you go you will cremate yourself and I will have wasted all this time and effort. On the other hand, it's perfectly obvious that I can't keep you here. He looked at the window which was closed. Moth, he said, I am going to do something for you which I've never before done for any of your kind. Stay still a moment.

With his left hand he tilted the wineglass; his right descended swiftly and covered the insect. He was amazed that it felt so firm beneath his fingers, not at all as he had thought, shapeless, gelatinous. It was almost like holding a very small bird. He put down the wineglass and stood up, carefully easing back his chair. He did not notice that the moth had crawled up the tunnel made by his forefinger and was almost out of his grasp. He walked across the room and as he reached out to open the window, the moth burst free. He was angry and swore at it. When it flew over his head, he put up his hands to dash it to the floor. Then he became embarrassed at his unreasonable outburst and sat down, wiping his hand on his jacket and thinking, What the hell, it's only a moth.

Imprisoned now by instinct alone, the insect came back to the candle. This time he did not interfere but he still felt sympathetic towards it. He watched it play tag with the flame and wished it luck for its courage and thought that perhaps he would have done it an injustice by putting it outside. While it was near the candle, the moth ceased to be an ugly thing, was, in fact, quite beautiful. The tatty wings, singed and healed in the flickering light, were coated with tarnished gold dust; the eyes gleamed like rubies. Again and again it descended in a whirlpool path. When the flame leapt up and licked it would break away, climb up and repeat the same movements, a dance of death that was part of its life.

As he watched, he felt guilty that he had despised it, and when it touched the flame for the last time, he was genuinely sorry. He leaned forward to examine the body at the base of the candlestick and couldn't help but think how dignified it looked, how much smaller and neater, now that it was still. He picked it up between his thumb and forefinger and placed it beside the flame, in the pool of melted wax below the wick.

Some time later, she came back into the room, shutting the door behind her.

'I didn't intend being so long,' she said. 'That girl has nothing better to do with her time —'

He knew that she was lying. 'It doesn't matter,' he said.

'Of course it matters. Haven't you missed me?' She moved her chair round the corner of the table so that it was touching his. 'Haven't you?'

She sat down and put her hand over his wrist. Her fingers were long and white, too large at the knuckles to be beautiful, but immensely capable. 'All right,' she said. 'Now tell me what's on your mind.'

'What do you mean?' he said, playing for time.

'You were going to tell me something before the phone went. You said it was important. Remember?'

'Oh that.' He was unprepared. The words he had turned on his tongue all day were trite and irrelevant, borrowed from fiction, and now, very remote.

'What was it?' she said. 'Tell me.'

He remembered that he had looked for this moment, but he hadn't expected that she would place it, deliberately, before him. She was at his side, watching, waiting for him to choose. He looked at the hand on his, and suddenly, his position was so clear that he wondered why he hadn't recognised it before. There was no choice. There never had been. Who and what she is, doesn't matter, he thought. She *is*. That's all that matters. And as long as she *is*, I can change nothing.

He glanced beyond her, at the room — her neat, prismatic room — and at the geometrical shadows that moved up against the walls. 'It wasn't important,' he said. 'I was going to tell you that I was leaving early.'

'Why?'

'I thought I'd better.'

'But you told me you had the weekend free. Didn't you say that she'd taken the car and gone to her sisters'?' She was smiling, a half-smile, as though she had known all the time what he had only just discovered.

'Yes, she did.'

'Then you don't have to go.'

'No,' he said. There was nothing else to say. He turned, seeking her. She pushed him away, gently but firmly, and got up to put a record on the gramophone. As she came back to her chair, she frowned, leaned across the table.

'What's that?' she indicated the candle.

'A moth,' he said.

She shrugged, 'Senseless brutes,' and sat down, half-closing her eyes to the opening bars of a Chopin waltz.

'I was going to put it out,' he said.

She opened her eyes. 'The candle?'

'No, I didn't think of that. I was going to open the window and let the moth go outside.'

For a few seconds her eyes searched his face, then the lids came down again and she gently swayed from side to side as though her attention had been completely given to the music.

But her hand was on his wrist and the bracelet of fingers had become so tight that he expected to see his blood under the points of her nails. He didn't move. The pain excited him and made him afraid.

After a long time she turned towards him. 'I'm glad you didn't,' she said.

'What?' He didn't understand her. The past had moved into the darkness on the other side of the window, and the present held nothing but the desire to possess and be consumed.

She leaned closer. 'I'm glad you didn't,' she repeated.

He hadn't the faintest idea what she was talking about.

# THE SILK

When Mr Blackie took bad again that autumn both he and Mrs Blackie knew that it was for the last time. For many weeks neither spoke of it; but the understanding was in their eyes as they watched each other through the days and nights. It was a look, not of sadness or despair, but of quiet resignation tempered with something else, an unnamed expression that is seen only in the old and the very young.

Their acceptance was apparent in other ways, too. Mrs Blackie no longer complained to the neighbours that the old lazy-bones was running her off her feet. Instead she waited on him tirelessly, stretching their pension over chicken and out-of-season fruits to tempt his appetite; and she guarded him so possessively that she even resented the twice-weekly visits from the district nurse. Mr Blackie, on the other hand, settled into bed as gently as dust. He had never been a man to dwell in the past, but now he spoke a great deal of their earlier days and surprised Mrs Blackie by recalling things which she, who claimed the better memory, had forgotten. Seldom did he talk of the present, and never in these weeks did he mention the future.

Then, on the morning of the first frost of winter, while Mrs Blackie was filling his hot water bottle, he sat up in bed, unaided, to see out the window. The inside of the glass was streaked with tears of condensation. Outside, the frost had made an oval frame of crystals through which he could see a row of houses and lawns laid out in front of them, like white carpets.

'The ground will be hard,' he said at last. 'Hard as nails.'

Mrs Blackie looked up quickly. 'Not yet,' she said.

'Pretty soon, I think.' His smile was apologetic.

She slapped the hot water bottle into its cover and tested it against her cheek. 'Lie down or you'll get a chill,' she said.

Obediently, he dropped back against the pillow, but as she moved about him, putting the hot water bottle at his feet, straightening the quilt, he stared at the frozen patch of window.

'Amy, you'll get a double plot, won't you?' he said. 'I wouldn't rest easy thinking you were going to sleep by someone else.'

'What a thing to say!' The corner of her mouth twitched. 'As if I would.'

'It was your idea to buy single beds,' he said accusingly.

'Oh, Herb —' She looked at the window, away again. 'We'll have a double plot,' she said. For a second or two she hesitated by his bed, then she sat beside his feet, her hands placed one on top of the other in her lap, in a pose that she always adopted when she had something important to say. She cleared her throat.

'You know, I've been thinking on and off about the silk.'

'The silk?' He turned his head towards her.

'I want to use it for your laying-out pyjamas.'

'No, Amy,' he said. 'Not the silk. That was your wedding present, the only thing I brought back with me.'

'What would I do with it now?' she said. When he didn't answer, she got up, opened the wardrobe door and took the camphorwood box from the shelf where she kept her hats. 'All these years and us not daring to take a scissors to it. We should use it sometime.'

'Not on me,' he said.

'I've been thinking about your pyjamas.' She fitted a key into the brass lock. 'It'd be just right.'

'A right waste, you mean,' he said. But there was no protest in his voice. In fact, it had lifted with a childish eagerness. He watched her hands as she opened the box and folded back layers of white tissue paper. Beneath them lay the blue of the silk. There was a reverent silence as she took it out and spread it under the light.

'Makes the whole room look different, doesn't it?' he said. 'I nearly forgot it looked like this.' His hands struggled free of the sheet and moved across the quilt. Gently, she picked up the blue material and poured it over his fingers.

'Aah,' he breathed, bringing it closer to his eyes. 'All the way from China.' He smiled. 'Not once did I let it out of me sight. You know that, Amy? There were those on board as would have pinched it quick as that. I kept it pinned round me middle.'

'You told me,' she said.

He rubbed the silk against the stubble of his chin. 'It's the birds that take your eye,' he said.

'At first,' said Mrs Blackie. She ran her finger over one of the peacocks that strutted in the foreground of a continuous landscape. They were proud birds, iridescent blue, with silver threads in their tails. 'I used to like them best, but after a while you see much more, just as fine, only smaller.' She pushed her glasses on to the bridge of her nose and leaned over the silk, her finger guiding her eyes over islands where waterfalls hung, eternally suspended, between pagodas and dark blue conifers, over flat lakes and tiny fishing boats, over mountains where the mists never lifted, and back again to a haughty peacock caught with one foot suspended over a rock. 'It's a work of art like you never see in this country,' she said.

Mr Blackie inhaled the scent of camphorwood. 'Don't cut it, Amy. It's too good for an old blighter like me.' He was begging her to contradict him.

'I'll get the pattern tomorrow,' she said.

The next day, while the district nurse was giving him his injection, she went down to the store and looked through a pile of pattern books. Appropriately, she chose a mandarin style with a high collar and piped cuffs and pockets. But Mr Blackie, who had all his life worn striped flannel in the conventional design, looked with suspicion at the pyjama pattern and the young man who posed so easily and shamelessly on the front of the packet.

'It's the sort them teddy bear boys have,' he said.

'Nonsense,' said Mrs Blackie.

'That's exactly what they are,' he growled. 'You're not laying me out in a lot of new-fangled nonsense.'

Mrs Blackie put her hands on her hips. 'You'll not have any say in the matter,' she said.

'Won't I just? I'll get up and fight — see if I don't.'

The muscles at the corner of her mouth twitched uncontrollably. 'All right, Herb, if you're so set against it —'

But now, having won the argument, he was happy. 'Get away with you, Amy. I'll get used to the idea.' He threw his lips back against his gums. 'Matter of fact, I like them fine. It's that nurse that done it. Blunt needle again.' He looked at the pattern. 'When d'you start?'

'Well —'

'This afternoon?'

'I suppose I could pin the pattern out after lunch.'

'Do it in here,' he said. 'Bring in your machine and pins and things and set them up so I can watch.'

She stood taller and tucked in her chin. 'I'm not using the machine,' she said with pride. 'Every stitch is going to be done by hand. My eyes mightn't be as good as they were once, mark you, but there's not a person on this earth can say I've lost my touch with a needle.'

His eyes closed in thought. 'How long?'

'Eh?'

'Till it's finished.'

17

She turned the pattern over in her hands. 'Oh — about three or four weeks. That is — if I keep at it.'

'No,' he said. 'Too long.'

'Oh Herb, you'd want a good job done, wouldn't you?' she pleaded.

'Amy —' Almost imperceptibly, he shook his head on the pillow.

'I can do the main seams on the machine,' she said, lowering her voice.

'How long?'

'A week,' she whispered.

When she took down the silk that afternoon, he insisted on an extra pillow in spite of the warning he'd had from the doctor about lying flat with his legs propped higher than his head and shoulders.

She plumped up the pillow from her own bed and put it behind his neck; then she unrolled her tape measure along his body, legs, arms, around his chest.

'I'll have to take them in a bit,' she said, making inch-high black figures on a piece of cardboard. She took the tissue-paper pattern into the kitchen to iron it flat. When she came back, he was waiting, wide-eyed with anticipation and brighter, she thought, than he'd been for many weeks.

As she laid the silk out on her bed and started pinning down the first of the pattern pieces, he described with painstaking attempts at accuracy, the boat trip home, the stop at Hong Kong, and the merchant who had sold him the silk.

'Most of his stuff was rubbish,' he said. 'You wouldn't look twice at it. This was the only decent thing he had and even then he done me. You got to argue with these devils. Beat them down, they told me. But there was others as wanted that silk and if I hadn't made up me mind there and then I'd have lost it.' He squinted at her hands. 'What are you doing now? You just put that bit down.'

'It wasn't right,' she said, through lips closed on pins. 'I have to

18

match it — like wallpaper.'

She lifted the pattern pieces many times before she was satisfied. Then it was evening and he was so tired that his breathing had become laboured. He no longer talked. His eyes were watering from hours of concentration; the drops spilled over his red lids and soaked into the pillow.

'Go to sleep,' she said. 'Enough's enough for one day.'

'I'll see you cut it out first,' he said.

'Let's leave it till the morning,' she said, and they both sensed her reluctance to put the scissors to the silk.

'Tonight,' he said.

'I'll make the tea first.'

'After,' he said.

She took the scissors from her sewing drawer and wiped them on her apron. Together they felt the pain as the blades met cleanly, almost without resistance, in that first cut. The silk would never again be the same. They were changing it, rearranging the pattern of fifty-odd years to form something new and unfamiliar. When she had cut out the first piece, she held it up, still pinned to the paper, and said, 'The back of the top.' Then she laid it on the dressing table and went on as quickly as she dared, for she knew that he would not rest until she had finished.

One by one the garment pieces left the body of silk. With each touch of the blades, threads sprang apart; mountains were divided, peacocks split from head to tail; waterfalls fell on either side of fraying edges. Eventually, there was nothing on the bed but a few shining snippets. Mrs Blackie picked them up and put them back in the camphorwood box, and covered the pyjama pieces on the dressing table with a cloth. Then she removed the extra pillow from Mr Blackie's bed and laid his head back in a comfortable position before she went into the kitchen to make the tea.

He was very tired the next morning but refused to sleep while she was working with the silk. She invented a number of excuses for putting it aside and leaving the room. He would sleep then, but never for long. No more than half an hour would pass and he would be calling her. She would find him lying awake and impatient for her to resume sewing.

In that day and the next, she did all the machine work. It was a tedious task, for first she tacked each seam by hand, matching the patterns in the weave so that the join was barely noticeable. Mr Blackie silently supervised every stitch. At times she would see him studying the silk with an expression that she still held in her memory. It was the look he'd given her in their courting days. She felt a prick of jealousy, not because she thought that he cared more for the silk than he did for her, but because he saw something in it that she didn't share. She never asked him what it was. At her age a body did not question these things or demand explanations. She would bend her head lower and concentrate her energy and attention into the narrow seam beneath the needle.

On the Friday afternoon, four days after she'd started the pyjamas, she finished the buttonholes and sewed on the buttons. She'd deliberately hurried the last of the hand sewing. In the four days Mr Blackie had become weaker, and she knew that the sooner the pyjamas were completed and put back in the camphorwood box out of sight, the sooner he would take an interest in food and have the rest he needed.

She snipped the last thread and put the needle in its case.

'That's it, Herb,' she said, showing him her work.

He tried to raise his head. 'Bring them over here,' he said.

'Well — what do you think?' As she brought the pyjamas closer, his eyes relaxed and he smiled.

'Try them on?' he said.

She shook her head. 'I got the measurements,' she said. 'They'll be the right fit.'

'Better make sure,' he said.

She hesitated but could find no reason for her reluctance. 'All right,' she said, switching on both bars of the electric heater and drawing it closer to his bed. 'Just to make sure I've got the buttons right.'

She peeled back the bedclothes, took off his thick pyjamas and put on the silk. She stepped back to look at him.

'Well, even if I do say so myself, there's no one could have done a better job. I could move the top button over a fraction, but apart from that they're a perfect fit.'

He grinned. 'Light, aren't they?' He looked down the length of his body and wriggled his toes. 'All the way from China. Never let it out of me sight. Know that, Amy?'

'Do you like them?' she said.

He sucked his lips in over his gums to hide his pleasure. 'All right. A bit on the tight side.'

'They are not, and you know it,' Mrs Blackie snapped. 'Never give a body a bit of credit, would you? Here, put your hands down and I'll change you before you get a chill.'

He tightened his arms across his chest. 'You made a right good job, Amy. Think I'll keep them on a bit.'

'No.' She picked up his thick pyjamas.

'Why not?'

'Because you can't,' she said. 'It — it's disrespectful. And the nurse will be here soon.'

'Oh, get away with you, Amy.' He was too weak to resist further but as she changed him, he still possessed the silk with his eyes. 'Wonder who made it?'

Although she shrugged his question away, it brought to her a definite picture of a Chinese woman seated in front of a loom surrounded by blue and silver silkworms. The woman was dressed from a page in a geographic magazine, and except for the oriental line of her eyelids, she looked like Mrs Blackie.

'D'you suppose there's places like that?' Mr Blackie asked.

She snatched up the pyjamas and put them in the box. 'You're the one that's been there,' she said briskly. 'Now settle down and rest or you'll be bad when the nurse arrives.'

The district nurse did not come that afternoon. Nor in the evening. It was at half-past three the following morning that her footsteps, echoed by the doctor's, sounded along the gravel path.

21

Mrs Blackie was in the kitchen, waiting. She sat straight-backed and dry-eyed, her hands placed one on top of the other in the lap of her dressing-gown.

'Mrs Blackie. I'm sorry —'

She ignored the nurse and turned to the doctor. 'He didn't say goodbye,' she said with an accusing look. 'Just before I phoned. His hand was over the side of the bed. I touched it. It was cold.'

The doctor nodded.

'No sound of any kind,' she said. 'He was good as gold last night.'

Again the doctor nodded. He put his hand, briefly, on her shoulder, then went into the bedroom. Within a minute he returned, fastening his leather bag and murmuring sympathy.

Mrs Blackie sat still, catching isolated words. Expected. Peacefully. Brave. They dropped upon her — neat, geometrical shapes that had no meaning.

'He didn't say goodbye.' She shook her head. 'Not a word.'

'But look, Mrs Blackie,' soothed the nurse. 'It was inevitable. You knew that. He couldn't have gone on —'

'I know, I know.' She turned away, irritated by their lack of understanding. 'He just might have said goodbye. That's all.'

The doctor took a white tablet from a phial and tried to persuade her to swallow it. She pushed it away; refused, too, the cup of tea that the district nurse poured and set in front of her. When they picked up their bags and went towards the bedroom, she followed them.

'In a few minutes,' the doctor said. 'If you'll leave us —'

'I'm getting his pyjamas,' she said. 'There's a button needs changing. I can do it now.'

As soon as she entered the room, she glanced at Mr Blackie's bed and noted that the doctor had pulled up the sheet. Quickly, she lifted the camphorwood box, took a needle, cotton, scissors, her spectacle case, and went back to the kitchen. Through the half-closed door she heard the nurse's voice, 'Poor old thing,' and she knew, instinctively, that they were not talking about her.

She sat down at the table to thread the needle. Her eyes were clear but her hands were so numb that for a long time they refused to work together. At last, the thread knotted, she opened the camphorwood box. The beauty of the silk was always unexpected. As she spread the pyjamas out on the table, it warmed her, caught her up and comforted her with the first positive feeling she'd had that morning. The silk was real. It was brought to life by the electric light above the table, so that every fold of the woven landscape moved. Trees swayed towards rippling water and peacocks danced with white fire in their tails. Even the tiny bridges —

Mrs Blackie took off her glasses, wiped them, put them on again. She leaned forward and traced her thumbnail over one bridge, then another. And another. She turned over the pyjama coat and closely examined the back. It was there, on every bridge; something she hadn't noticed before. She got up, and from the drawer where she kept her tablecloths, she took out her magnifying glass.

As the bridge in the pattern of the silk grew, the figure, which had been no larger than an ant, became a man.

Mrs Blackie forgot about the button, and the murmur of voices in the bedroom. She brought the magnifying glass nearer her eyes.

It was a man and he was standing with one arm outstretched, on the highest span between two islands. Mrs Blackie studied him for a long time, then she straightened up and smiled. Yes he was waving. Or perhaps, she thought, he was beckoning to her.

# HOUSE WITH A VIEW

As soon as she saw the house, Marion knew she must buy it. It was a gem of a place, pink and white plaster set on a side of the hill half-way between the road and the sea, a small house made smaller by an untamed garden.

Neat section and small plaster dwelling of immaculate appearance, the land agent had said, building an image of a pink war memorial on city council lawns. Quite wrong. The house appeared to be in good condition, yes, but there was a certain shabbiness about it, a lack of pretence suggesting that it was there for comfort rather than admiration. For Marion it had all the warmth and familiarity of a forgotten dream.

'I thought there was a garage,' said Hugh, pulling on the hand-brake.

'Does it matter?' she said.

'Oh no,' he said. 'It doesn't matter at all. We just leave eight hundred pounds' worth of car out on the road.'

She turned away from his disapproval and pressed her face against the car window. 'Look down there. Just look at the water. When he said it had a view of the harbour I didn't think it was like this.'

'I told him I wasn't interested in a place without a garage,' said Hugh. 'You heard me say that, didn't you?'

'Yes, I heard. He probably forgot.' Thank goodness, she added in a breath that barely misted the glass. She opened the door and stepped out on to the footpath. 'Well? Are you coming?'

He laughed as though the request was beyond all reason. 'Not on your life. I'm no bloody mountain goat.' And he waved his cigarette at her. 'You go. Go on, have a look through and I'll wait here.'

She stood by the car, unable to think of anything to say. Already she had said too much. She looked behind her at the white fence corsetting a row of fat coprosma bushes, at the overgrown mailbox, the path that dropped away in a series of narrow steps.

'I can't go on my own.'

He shrugged. 'Then hop in. We're wasting time.'

'Please, Hugh.'

'I am not looking at that house,' he said, emphasising each syllable with a nod. 'It's right out as far as we're concerned and the land agent knew it.'

Marion turned away. As she pulled on her gloves she said, 'If I have to go on my own, I will buy it.' Then she walked quickly through the gate, too embarrassed to look back at him. Never, she had told herself, never would she use the money as a weapon against Hugh. Now, as easily as that, she had done it, broken her vow a fortnight after it had been made.

When she heard the car door slam, she would not allow herself to recognise victory. She went on down the steps, very slowly, watching her shoes.

'Are you mad?' he said, taking her arm. 'A place like this? You know what your father would have said.'

His habit of using her dead father in his arguments always infuriated her. No wave of indignation washed away self-reproach, and she said, 'No need to shout, Hugh,' in as normal a voice as she could manage.

'You'd have to be clean round the bend to live here,' he said.

Why did he always have to be so difficult? If only, just once, she thought, she could have her way without all the unpleasantness. She looked at the yellow clay that sucked around her feet. 'But we've been through dozens of house. Why not this one?'

'You've already made up your mind,' said Hugh. 'I know you and your obsessions — turtles on the refrigerator, damned old clock that'll never go in a million years, that thing you call a painting —'

She was silent while he fed her loves, one by one, through his adding machine.

'Five and a half thousand, remember. And you'll be in it the rest of your life.'

'Yes, I know,' she said.

The path below the steps was gravel-filled and overlaid with shells. Whether the woman heard their footsteps or whether she had been watching through one of the back windows, Marion didn't know, but before Hugh could knock, the door swung open on a brown frock and felt slippers.

'Yes?' The face was all nose and eyes, dark eyes with dry, hooded lids, and there was a row of black feathers on the top lip.

'Mrs — ah —' Hugh had been startled into losing the name.

'Butler,' she said, folding her arms.

'Mrs Butler, we've come from Mr Heyworth. He couldn't bring us himself —'

'I know, it's the steps,' said the woman. 'He's got gout.' She snapped her eyes at Marion. 'But he phoned and said you were coming.'

'Would it be convenient for us to see through?' Marion asked.

'Steps worry you?' The woman didn't move from the doorway. 'Some folks came the other day. I spent half an hour or so on them, then they said the steps were too steep.'

'If you want a view you've got to expect a bit of a climb,' Marion said. Encouraged by Hugh's silence, she added, 'We don't mind.'

The woman's expression didn't change but she moved aside. 'It's not a big place,' she said. 'Not over-flash, but it's comfortable.'

Marion walked in first, up the concrete step and into the back porch. She stopped and held out her hands.

'You like this sort of thing?' said the woman.

Half a dozen ferns in baskets hung from the ceiling above their heads. Round the walls, tiered shelves supported more plants: ivy, pelargoniums, orchids, heavy-scented hyacinths and succulents Marion had never seen before. A long window box had been nailed to the ledge. In it, fifteen to twenty cacti squatted, like old men, in the sun.

'Yes,' said Marion. 'Oh yes. I do have some —'

'Quite a collection,' said the woman. 'They belonged to Arthur, my late husband. He used to spend hours out here, fussing about, repotting.' She leaned forward to destroy a cobweb. 'The plants go with the house.'

'You're not taking them?' said Marion.

'No. If the new owner doesn't want them he can sell them. Put an ad in the paper and I daresay they'd fetch a bit.' She stepped past Marion and opened the door. 'Kitchen's in here.'

The kitchen was white, all white, and as clean as a doctor's surgery. Marion thought of the kitchen in the flat, hardly bigger than a cupboard, where the sink leaked and mildew flowered in the darkness. Here, with so much light and space — She put out her hand to stroke the white stove and found her fingers curling possessively over the handle of the oven door.

'New stove, you see,' said the woman. 'Arthur put in the stainless steel sink and bench three years ago and that extra cupboard.'

Marion glanced at Hugh. He was standing apart from them, deliberately remote.

'Did Mr Butler do the interior decorating too?' she asked.

'Oh yes,' said the woman. 'Gardens and all. Arthur was very good round the place. He had artistic hands.'

Marion followed her into the living room. She felt that she

should, in some way, acknowledge the woman's loss, yet she was afraid to offer anything as personal as sympathy.

'He's made it all so nice,' she said at last. 'You'll be sorry to leave it.'

The woman folded her arms and turned, almost aggressively. 'No I won't,' she said, her eyelids snapping open and shut with her mouth. 'I don't mind telling you it's too much for one person. Have you looked round the section, seen the garden? Have you? And I'm getting too old for those steps.'

'You'll miss the view,' Marion said. She leaned against the window and stared down at the sleeping sea. When a storm awoke it, those rocks would be covered in foam.

'That's what my late husband used to say.' She said 'late husband' as though accusing him of unpunctuality. For a few seconds she stared at Marion without blinking, then she went on briskly, 'You go through here to the bedrooms.'

Hugh did not follow them into the main bedroom. He watched from the doorway, his face strained with patience.

'There's your view again,' said the woman waving her hand at the window. 'Plenty of wardrobe space here. See the light fittings? Seventeen pounds for this room alone.'

Adding machine, thought Marion. She looked at Hugh, but there was no flicker of interest in his face.

'Hugh, your desk could go in this alcove. See the light?'

'Yes dear,' he said without looking.

The second bedroom was smaller, painted and decorated in green. The light from the single side-window was filtered through the leaves of a gum tree making the whole room as dim as an underwater cave. Marion could easily imagine the furniture floating down through it and settling like a handful of shells. In fact, for a ridiculous moment, she saw herself lifting the bed and holding it up to her ear.

Hugh spoke suddenly. 'Bit overgrown, isn't it?' he said in his ha-ha voice.

'That tree should be cut right out,' said the woman. She

looked at Hugh. 'You could make short work of it,' she said.

It was useless, Marion wanted to tell her, quite useless baiting the trap with flattery. Hugh suspected even the smallest compliment.

'I'd leave the tree as it is,' she said.

'Well? Satisfied?' he asked later as they went up the path to the car. He was taking the steps two at a time and so fast that she could spare no more than one word.

'Yes,' she gasped.

While she was struggling over the last of the slope, he stood by the car, holding the door open and laughing. 'I'd like to see you do that every day.'

She reached the footpath and looked back at the sea, still calm, unruffled in its sleep. But here was her heart, flopping about like a dying fish and her legs feeling as though they were eighty years old. She put her arm out to Hugh and he helped her to the car.

'Come on,' he said, patting her on the back. 'We'll have a cup of tea before I go back to work.'

He talked quickly, cheerfully, all the way into town, putting as much effort into the conversation, she thought, as he had into the climb. Sooner or later she would have to tell him.

'Pity I've got to go back to work,' he said, as they waited for the lights to change.

Later, she decided. He wouldn't be able to raise his voice in a crowded tearoom.

She was right. He didn't shout at her. They argued and threatened with the voices of strangers discussing the weather.

'If I can't get that house, I'll stay where I am,' she said, muffling the words with her cup.

'We've given our notice,' he said. 'The new tenants are waiting to move in.'

'Then I'll live in a tent,' she said.

'All right, you bloody well will,' he said.

The calm that followed was an uneasy one. Hugh didn't mention the house again that day. When he came home from work he took his dinner into the lounge and ate it in front of the television set. In the morning he had his breakfast behind the paper and left for work half an hour earlier than usual.

Almost as soon as he had gone, Marion went through the flat, stocktaking, rearranging, fitting their possessions into a new setting. Strange that the furniture she had been collecting for seventeen years should suddenly come together in complete harmony with a house she'd known less than twenty-four hours.

At lunch-time she phoned the land agent, said she would call to see him next day; then, in the afternoon, she began to pack — small things that would not be missed, spare cutlery, linen, china. By five o'clock she had three boxes stowed away in the back of her wardrobe.

She was prepared for another scene with Hugh. Her mind was made up so completely that nothing he could say would alter it. But what she hadn't anticipated was his sudden change in mood. He came up the path like a school-boy, his footsteps loud and confident, and he shouted, 'Hullo love!' at the back door.

Not once during dinner did he mention the house. Could it have been sold? No, there was no one else. What then?

It came out while he was helping her to dry the dishes. 'You know that place we saw yesterday afternoon?' he said, as though she could have forgotten.

She looked sideways at him. 'What about it?'

'I was talking to Heyworth today. He was telling me about the husband, Arthur Butler.'

'Yes?' she said, curious but still secure.

'He died two months ago.'

Only two months! She kept her head down and went on washing the plates.

'He committed suicide.'

Everything inside her stopped and the water turned cold on her hands. Late husband. There he was in the gum tree, his feet swinging against the bedroom window. She could see him in the porch. His blood scented the hyacinths. One by one the bubbles in the dishwater burst.

'How?' she whispered.

'Overdose of sleeping tablets,' said Hugh. 'The land agent said he'd been ill for years — mentally, that is. Must have been hard for his wife.'

'Yes,' she said, her voice pitched high in a silly giggle. 'Yes, it must have been. Still, I don't see that it makes any difference to us and the house.'

But it did make a difference. All the difference in the world.

# THE WOMAN NEXT DOOR

S ix, perhaps seven, the child of the photograph, solid against the blur of a city, unsmiling in black and white. She was old enough then to have learned that black and white were the non-colours, the everything and nothing that had no place in rainbows. She also knew that God was white and the Devil black, while the in-between tones, the greys of the street in the photograph, belonged to War.

And the child knew about War. It lay all the way between everything and nothing and covered the city so that no matter where one went there was no escaping it. It was a grey smoke that filled the air they had to breathe.

At school she watched the boys draw aeroplanes that resembled ducks laying eggs in flight, and she would feel the metal disc, named, numbered, on the string about her neck, and look up at the sky above the playground.

In the home the blinds were secured when sirens sounded, cups rattled on their hooks when trucks rolled past. Every morning the newspaper was unfolded over the kitchen table, plates covered with grey pictures, and above the toaster there was a voice that said, 'This is the BBC London calling. Here is the news.'

The child learned much by remaining silent through mealtime conversations but she never discovered who had thrown stones through Mrs Gessner's front windows. No one seemed to know. No one seemed particularly interested. Nor could she find out where Mr Gessner had gone. Certainly he wasn't fighting with the soldiers, for one day someone, an aunt, uncle perhaps, someone had said, 'Well, what would you do if they told you to go over and shoot your relatives?' And a grey sort of silence had settled in the room.

Their neighbour had not appeared to be disturbed by the breaking of the windows. While the workmen cleared the fragments of glass and put in new panes, Mrs Gessner carried on working in her garden. Her face under the straw hat was flat and expressionless. The unlaced boots never hurried. Up and down the rows, day after day, those broad, freckled hands pulled weeds from the flowerbeds.

The child didn't speak but she often watched. She would lie in the grass on her own side of the fence and press her face against the palings, thrilled by her own daring. Dirty Hun, they'd said at school. Watch out or she'll get you. Spy, spy, string her up high. She would watch every movement and when it seemed likely that the brim of the straw hat was going to tilt in her direction she would put her head down and crawl backwards until she was behind her grandfather's bean frame, and she would stay there until the squat figure had moved away.

But nothing happened to her. Nothing. After a while the children at school lost interest in the story about the sounds of breaking glass in the middle of the night, and the mystery woman next door took on an ordinariness that defied the child's imagination. It did not seem right that a spy should put out tins of dripping for the birds or scratch down the back of her dress with a knitting needle. The child grew bolder. It was no longer satisfying to hide in the grass and stare. She came out into the open, walked along the fence, sometimes stood still and leaned on it. She met the woman's eyes, smiled when she smiled, even said hello.

Promise not to tell a living soul, she said to anyone at school who would listen. I talked to the spy.

Once she accepted a bunch of dahlias from the garden and was thrilled to find two earwigs in the petals. She took them to school next morning in a bottle and everyone looked. Oh yes, they were German earwigs, all right.

Then the child's father was killed. The man in the photograph on the mantelpiece was drowned at sea and everything about the child's house changed. It became quiet. People walked in it as though they no longer knew the way, and they talked in tired voices. Sometimes they would not leave the child alone. Sometimes they forgot she was there. The grey of war sat at the dinner table with them and curled up on their plates, making everything taste like the dead earth under houses.

The child took to playing in the garden next door.

Years later she would not be able to remember her first visit but soon she was crossing the fence so regularly that Mrs Gessner cut down some of the palings to make it easier for her. And because the child was older now, and in a new class at school, she no longer felt the need to confide in other children or relatives, for that matter.

On warm afternoons she would sit under the apple tree by a mound of green fruit, or wander along the borders popping fuchsia buds, or kneel on the path urging snails to compete on a brick raceway. Mrs Gessner used to bring out the canvas chairs and they would sit, the two of them, drinking milk and eating biscuits with currants and lemon in them.

Then there were the days when they went into the house and the cool dark kitchen with its smells of apples and firewood and caraway seeds, and the child would climb up into the rocking chair, wriggling into a nest of cushions, while Mrs Gessner brought out the music box. It was of dark wood, carved, with a lid which framed trees and dancing deer; and when the lid was opened it was easy to tell why the deer danced like that, for from the emptiness of the box came a song of little bells, the same tune over and over until the lid was closed and Mrs Gessner was wiping the box on her apron and smiling, ya, is beautiful? Is beautiful? and the child was holding out her hands, begging for the music again.

Perhaps she talked to her family about the music box. Later, she was unable to remember that either. But it seemed that the family, slow with grief, had dragged their thinking to the gap in the wooden fence. As an uncle nailed up the boards, they took the child before her grandfather who wanted to know how long she had been going next door. How long was long? Weeks? Years? She didn't know. Then Grandfather talked about King and country and the child's father. He talked to her seriously as though she were already grown up, the way he spoke to her uncles, only kinder. He had steel-rimmed glasses, and grey hairs growing out of his nose. She knew that she would give her dead father a pain that was much worse than drowning, if she ever went next door again.

Some time after that, Mrs Gessner moved away from the street. The child didn't see her leave. She came home from school and was met by Grandfather who gave her a brown paper parcel. Inside was the music box. The woman left it for the little girl, he said. She meant you, he said.

The child didn't know what to say. She felt as though she had been caught doing something wrong.

You know what your father would want you to do, Grandfather said.

Of course she knew. And as she put the music box on the fire, the aunts and uncle put their arms round her and told her she was a real little heroine, and that pleased her; but most of all she was pleased that she had made her father, who was living with the angels, very proud of his daughter.

# RURAL DELIVERY

The boy lay across the back seat of the station wagon, counting the bends in the road by the pressure on his feet or the top of his head. He was wearing felt slippers over woollen socks but his head was bare, hot and slightly aching, and when his father made a fast left turn the weight on his skull made white lights in front of his eyes.

His eyes hurt more than his head or throat in spite of the dullness of the day. If he stared at the window too long the lines of rain scratched him through the glass and he had to pull the blanket over his face to find darkness.

He had felt like this yesterday at school but it had seemed worse then with the noise of the classroom, questions pecking at him from every direction, and finally the crying with eyes and nose running down his arm and onto the desk.

Today he had his father's handkerchief.

Lying flat against the pillow he was unable to see his father in the driver's seat, but the stops were frequent, sometimes less than a minute apart, and each time his father got out there was some joke about ducks or mud, or a story about the farmer whose name appeared on the mail-box. For a moment his father's face would be large above him, laughing and spilling drops of rain, then the door would slam and he'd be pressed back in the seat with the sound of water rushing under the tyres.

Bread, newspapers, green canvas bags of mail, even through his cold they reached him, not as separate odours but one which was as warm and personal as the smell inside his schoolbag.

'Dad?' He had been forbidden to sit up. He put his hands behind his head and raised it until he could see the yellow hood of his father's parka. 'Hey Dad?'

'What?'

'You know at school that Jason Morris? He said I was a liar. He said nobody's been on every road in New Zealand. Like I was just skiting.' He swallowed to wet his throat. 'I told him he was dumb. I said it was even the little roads not on the maps and the ones that only went half-way to places. That's right, isn't it Dad? You went on every single one?'

'You bet your sweet life I did.' His father slapped both hands on top of the steering wheel and straightened his arms, pushing back against the seat. 'The whole lot, Chief. Every road in the country right down to Stewart Island where they all wear grass skirts and hardly know what a car looks like. That kid in school, you tell him to stick a pin in the map — anywhere, you tell him — and I'll show him my own personal tread marks.'

'And not just trucks, eh Dad? Big artics and petrol tankers and ready-mix concrete —'

'Every one of them, Chief. I've carried anything and everything on just about any set of wheels you'd care to name. Including people, of course, and that I reckon's the hardest by a long chalk, a busload of people. Oh, it'd all be fine enough if you had that little green man driving alongside you, but if he wasn't there, then that was it, Chief. That was when you wished you had a crate of steers or a load of old potatoes. I tell you I'd rather drive a petrol tanker through a forest fire than be stranded with a busful of human souls. Specially tourists. Don't talk to me about tourist coaches. I've seen them all and there were things happened that'd make me sob again in the telling. Saints alive! Now look what we've done!'

He braked so suddenly that the boy hurt his elbow against the door handle. The engine whined in reverse and the tail of the station wagon slewed towards a white mail-box. There were black letters on it but it was a long name and the boy's eyes got sore before he could work it out.

'That was close,' said his father. 'You wouldn't get a meaner old devil than this one. If I forgot his bread and paper, you know what he'd do, don't you? Set his bull on me. And heaven preserve us, you've never seen horns the likes of that before. Great brute of a thing. It'd rip this buggy open like a can of spaghetti in two seconds flat.'

'You're kidding,' said the boy. He pulled the blanket up round his chin, partly because of the draught from the open door, and sat up. In front of him there was a driveway with a house set far back in a clump of trees. On either side the paddocks were flat and full of sheep which nibbled grass as though they didn't know it was raining. Only a few near the road bothered to lift their heads and stare.

The boy's father opened the mail-box, threw in a loaf and a newspaper, closed it again, all with a quick crackle of yellow sleeve.

Rain was pencilled over everything. The driveway was flooded, a hump of clay and grass between two lines of brown water. Along the hump several geese waddled towards the house.

The boy turned his head. A blackbird landed on the post near his window, flicked its tail, flew away again. There was no sign of the bull. He yawned and lay back, his head fitted into the dent on his pillow, and counted the sweeps of the windscreen wipers. He was good at counting. He could count better than anyone else in his class.

Eighty-seven, eighty-eight — he raised his head again. 'You wait. I'm going to tell that Jason Morris it's him that's the liar.'

'Who?' said father.

'Jason Morris. That kid at school — you know.'

'Oh him.' His father nodded slowly. 'I know how you feel, Chief. Believe me, I know. But a liar's an awful bad thing to call a man. If I were you I'd just rest content with the knowing of it. Like what your mother used to say. When people talk bad about others, she said, it wasn't others they was judging but themselves. I'd go along with that, Chief. I'd reckon it wasn't too far out.'

The boy stared at the window and counted until the light made him blink. 'I told the kids at school my mother was dead.'

His father's head turned. 'Why in God's name?'

'Dunno.'

'Ah — come on now. You'd have to remember why you said a thing like that.'

'I don't know. I just did. I just said it.'

'David, there has to be a reason. People don't go around saying their mothers are dead when they're not. That's terrible. I mean, supposing she were to hear about it. How do you think she'd feel? Her own son talking her down into the grave like that —'

'She won't. You said she went back to Ireland.'

'There's ways people have of finding out even if they're on the other side of the earth. You shouldn't have said it. I've told you before, time and time again, there's things you won't understand until you're well growed up —'

The boy wished he'd kept quiet. He hadn't realise his father would make such a fuss, nor did he know why he'd told his classmates she was dead. There had been no good reason — except that it was easy to say.

His father stopped talking about it at the next mail-box and after that started making jokes again. He began his whistling too, not ordinary tunes but bird calls, warbles, high-pitched trills, his cheeks going in and out like the throat of a thrush. The boy sat up within range of the rear-vision mirror and when he knew he'd been seen he edged forward and put his arms across the top of his father's seat. As they braked at the entrance of another driveway, he asked if he could come through to the front.

39

'You're not supposed to be sitting up at all,' said his father. 'Lie down.'

'Oh Dad!'

'Go on now, lie right down like I said. You know what'll happen? You'll have a dreadful seizure and your face'll get hotter than hell, so hot your brain'll melt like a little ice-cream and run out your nose.'

'It won't!'

'Won't it just? I wouldn't be too smart if I were you. See now, you're getting redder all the time.' He put out his hand and rested his palm on the boy's forehead. 'You feeling all right?'

'I'm okay,' said the boy.

'Hungry?'

He shook his head.

'How about thirsty?'

The boy nodded.

'I'll get you a drink. That lunch-stop I mentioned, it's only a few miles away. Six more deliveries, then I'll get you anything you fancy — orange, milk, lemonade, you only have to say.'

The boy put his hand in his dressing-gown pocket. 'I brought my own money.'

'Money?' His father laughed. 'Saints alive, there's no shop out here. Did you think I meant a shop? There's not as much as a service station in these parts. No, this is just a place where I have my lunch now and then.' As he started to drive again, he said, 'You'll get on well with her. She's a good sort.'

'Who?' said the boy.

'The lady who gives us lunch, of course. She's got a lot of dogs down there. You'll hear them yapping their heads off before we're any way stopped — big ones, little ones, some of the funniest breeds you ever set eyes on.'

The boy lay back on the pillow. 'Do you go there lots?'

'No. Once or twice. It's too bad you've got the snuffles or you could be having a good look round the kennels. There's one dog with so much hair on it, you don't know which end is which, and that's a fact.'

'Tell me about the buses,' said the boy.

'Which ones?'

'You know. About tourists and things that happen.'

'Oh that,' said his father. 'You mean when the little green man deserts you in the middle of the night on the Lewis Pass with your power steering gone and six foot of snow and 38 Japanese who don't have a word of the Queen's English amongst them? Is that what you mean?'

'Yes, yes.' He propped himself up on one elbow. 'Tell me about that.'

'Well — it's an awful long story, Chief, a good eight-miler, I'd say. And the telling of it would be terrible thirsty work. We'll keep it for the road home.'

'Tell me a little story.'

'Not on an empty stomach.'

'Please? Dad?'

'After lunch.'

The boy lay down and turned his face to the back seat. His stomach itched. He kicked the blanket away but was still too hot. And when he scratched his stomach, it hurt.

'She's a nice lady,' said his father. 'You tell her what you want — a lemonade, coke, chocolate milk — and she'll get it for you. You'll like her.'

The boy said nothing. He reached for the blanket, pulled it over his head and lay still, pretending to sleep.

Perhaps he did doze a minute or two, for the woman's voice came on him suddenly, surprising him out of some place hot and distant. They were no longer moving. The engine had stopped and so had the drumming of rain. There was only her voice coming in from outside, touching him until he was listening.

'He should be in bed,' she was saying. 'On a day like this? Oh Joe, you must be out of your mind.'

'I couldn't leave him on his own. The lady who looks after him Saturday mornings, she's working, you see. I didn't have any choice.'

The boy kept his eyes closed as his father drew the blanket back from his face.

'He's very flushed.' The woman's voice was closer.

'He's got a real snorter, but I wrapped him up warm enough. He'll come to no harm.'

'He's too warm. Have you taken his temperature? Joe, he's burning up. It's more than a cold. Look — how long's he had that redness behind the ears?'

'First I've noticed. Looks like a bit of a rash.'

'Measles,' she said.

'You reckon?' His father was pulling at the blanket again. 'Come on, Chief, wake up. There's a lad, roll over and let's have a good look at you.'

The boy groaned and fluttered his eyelids.

'I say it's German measles,' said the woman.

'David?' said his father.

'What?' The boy decided to wake up. His father was kneeling on the front seat and leaning over him. He looked different, his hair combed, the grey jersey instead of the yellow parka, and he was talking a different way — as though he had borrowed someone else's voice and was being very careful with it. The woman watched through the half-open window. Her hair was done in pigtails but she was old, about thirty, and she wore a shirt with cowboys and lassoos on it.

It wasn't raining.

'David, this is Mrs Turner, the lady I was telling you about.'

'You poor kid,' she said. 'That's what it is. You've got measles.'

'Mrs Turner's getting you that drink. And what about a bite to eat now? A sandwich?'

The boy shook his head.

'He won't want to eat,' said the woman. 'Plenty of liquids, that's what he needs. Diluted orange juice with glucose.' She looked at the boy. 'Do you want ice in it, David?'

He nodded.

The boy's father was opening the back door. 'Now, don't try

to walk or anything funny, Chief. That's what dads are for. Roll yourself tight in the rug —'

'You can't bring him inside,' said the woman.

The boy's father looked at her.

'It's German measles, Joe. I've never had German measles. I'm sorry, he can't come into the house.'

'It's not the flaming smallpox!' his father said in his own voice.

'Nearly as bad,' she said.

'But you're not — you know.'

'What's that got to do with it?' She turned to the boy. 'You understand, David, what you've got is very catching. I mean very, very catching. You feel bad enough, but when adults get it, it's a whole lot more serious. Much worse. David, I'm going to get some orange drink for you. And your father's sandwiches. And I'm bringing them out here to the car. Then I think your father should take you straight home.'

The boy's father scratched the back of his neck and looked as though he was going to laugh. 'Now, wait a minute. Look, we haven't got ourselves a problem. I'll bring his drink out and then we'll have lunch inside, the two of us.'

'Leave David out here on his own?'

'We'll not exactly be deserting him. Will we, Chief? I mean, we'll be sitting in the kitchen not ten yards away.'

'You can't,' she said. 'You can't leave him.'

'He stayed outside the Post Office while I sorted the mail this morning,' he said.

'Joe, it's not right,' she said and she turned away.

'What can possibly happen —'

'I'm sorry,' she said.

The boy's father stood at the rear of the wagon staring after her, while the boy counted her footsteps. As she moved beyond his window he stopped counting to ask, 'Can I sit up now?'

'I suppose so,' said his father.

They had parked close to a large house. On either side were white painted walls and, in front, a carport containing a blue

Volkswagen and a mud-spattered motorbike. The woman was walking through the side of the carport to a brown door.

For the first time the boy became aware of the barking of dogs. There must have been dozens of them and yet they were so far away they sounded like a chorus of insects. 'Where are the kennels?' he asked.

His father didn't answer. He was staring at the house and softly tapping his fingers on the roof of the station wagon, his eyes half-shut as though he were dreaming.

'I can hear the dogs,' said the boy.

His father stopped tapping and smiled at him. He came inside and sat on the edge of the seat, one leg still out the door.

'Feeling better already, aren't you?'

The boy smiled back.

'I told you she was a nice lady.'

The boy nodded. He put his hand inside his dressing-gown and scratched his stomach.

'Now look, Chief, you and me — we both know that fair's fair. You wouldn't want me missing out on a decent lunch just because you're sick. And you heard what she said. I did my best but she doesn't want you in there while you got the measles. That's fair too. But I don't have the measles, do I now?'

The boy shook his head.

'And I know *you* won't object if I have a decent lunch sitting at a table.'

He shook his head again. 'I don't mind.'

'It's her,' his father said. 'You know how women are about these things. They make an awful fuss at times. I think you'll have to tell her when she comes out. Will you, Chief? Just say you're quite all right and you want to go to sleep. You need the rest. Tell her it's not easy sleeping on these bumpy roads. Can you remember that?'

The boy nodded.

'For your old Dad?'

'Yes,' said the boy.

His father ruffled his hair. 'I'll see what's keeping her,' he said.

The boy watched as he marched across the yard towards the door at the end of the carport, wide steps, hands in pockets, whistling. He went into the house without knocking, closed the door behind him.

No sound came from the house but beyond it, almost at the edge of listening, the barking and yelping of dogs never stopped for an instant.

The boy watched the brown door, counting to make it open. At one-hundred-and-seventy-one they both came out together, his father carrying a tray, laughing a lot, talking in that voice, and she a bit behind him with her head down.

His father came up to the wagon and beckoned the boy to look. 'What did I tell you?' he laughed, showing a white cloth, a paper napkin, a glass and a plastic jug full of juice with pips at the bottom and ice cubes on the top.

The woman walked to the other side of them but didn't come too close. She stooped to window level. 'Yes, I think you are a bit better. Less like a boiled beet. perhaps it was the blanket round your face. Is your throat dry? Poor kid, I'll bet you've got a raging thirst.'

She was right. He drank two glasses of the juice straight off, gulping and gasping, scarcely tasting it. His father poured a third and said, 'Does that make a difference?'

He took the glass and fished out a pip, then he sipped with his face down over the rim.

'How do you feel now?'

He didn't answer.

'Good, eh? I'll bet that's the sweetest drink you've ever tasted. You know how many oranges got squeezed to make that lot?'

Without a word the boy handed back the still full glass. He glanced at the woman. She wasn't looking at him but at his father, shaking her head and rounding her mouth to the shape of no.

'He's fine, he just told me. Didn't you, Chief?'

The boy was silent.

'He said all he wanted was a bit of a snooze. Right, David? Isn't that what you told me?'

'Joe, stop bullying the boy!'

'I'm not bullying him for heaven's sake. Hey! Cat got your tongue? Tell her. Tell her what you told me. What was it you said about wanting to go back to sleep?'

The boy didn't look at his father. He started to cough and the tears came, prickling at first, then a real flow as the coughing hurt his throat. He put his arms across his stomach and rocked back and forth. 'I want to go home.'

For a moment no one said anything; then his father put the glass back on the tray and handed it to the woman. She took the tray at arm's length and said, 'Just the jug. Joe, you take the glass.'

'Oh bloody hell!' said his father. He reached across the tray and tipped the orange juice out on the ground, then he brought his arm back and threw the glass right over the carport roof.

The boy didn't hear it land.

The woman tidied the things on the tray as though the glass had never been there, while the boy's father got into the car and started the engine.

'Joe, you'll let me know, won't you?' called the woman.

'Don't worry,' he shouted back. 'I'll let you know all right.'

She stood in front of the carport and watched as they reversed down the drive. The boy thought he might wave, and would have if his father had, but instead he held on to the back of the front seat with both hands.

At the end of the drive his father turned the wheels in a spray of muddy water, then took off so fast that the boy was pushed down on to the back seat. He lay where he had fallen for a while, then he got up on one elbow and said, 'I felt sick.'

'Sure,' said his father.

'I felt as sick as anything.' He moistened his lips. 'You know what? I got spots all over my stomach.'

The father didn't comment.

The boy sat up and undid his dressing-gown, then his pyjama jacket. He pulled up his vest and touched the red lumps on his skin. He had them everywhere, millions of them all over his body. He fastened his buttons again. 'Dad?'

A grunt came from the front seat.

'What about that time in the bus?'

'What about it?' said his father.

'You were going to tell me.'

There was a pause. 'I've forgotten.'

'No, you haven't. About the little green man and the time you got stuck in the snow.'

'What little green man?' His father's voice was angry. 'There's no such thing as a little green man. That's a load of old rubbish!'

The boy leaned sideways to look at his father's face in the rear-vision mirror. He watched it for a while, then he lay down on the seat with his pillow and blanket, and counted. After a few miles he went to sleep.

# GOD LOVES YOU,
# MISS ROSEWATER

He had planted barely half a row of potatoes when the preaching lady came round the back of the house with her bag of brochures and her terribly bright smile.

'Mr Bennett, isn't it? Perfect morning to be out-of-doors.'

'Indeed, indeed.' He put down the bucket of seed potatoes and glanced behind him at the tool-shed. it was much too late to hide.

'What a really magnificent garden you have here!'

He knew the woman by sight. She came at the same time nearly every Sunday morning at an hour when he was usually in bed surrounded by papers, the wreckage of breakfast and screaming kids who had to be hushed for the doorbell. Not that he ever went to the door. He made Hazel go. 'For your own good,' he'd tell her, pinching her on the backside until she was off her side of the bed, furious; and then, while she called him names and the children looked on hoping for a real fight, he'd say, 'It takes a woman to deal with a woman.'

He believed that, believed it with all his being. He was not a liberated man. He still suffered from a debilitating code of chivalry which made him a doormat for any saleswoman.

The preaching lady's heels clicked on the path between the rows of red-currant bushes. Her dress, years out of fashion, stopped an inch or so above her knees and she wore white gloves which were curled like fern fronds, one at her chest, the other round the strap of her bag. Her face was very plain.

'I trust I'm not disturbing you.' She was out of breath as though she'd been exercising. 'We haven't met yet but I know your wife. My name's Gilwater, Mrs Heather Gilwater. I have interrupted you, haven't I?'

'No, no, it's all right.'

He wondered why she deliberately held her voice at child's pitch. The sound was thin and delicate and it fluttered urgently like wings in a cobweb. Yet there was nothing frail or timid about her eyes. They shone with an aggressive kind of joy.

He winced without sound and wiped his hands on his trousers.

'I went to the front door and your little boy answered. He said you were in the garden, said I was to go round the back way.'

So it was Hazel's doing. He looked at the kitchen windows and imagined her watching, doubled over in her dressing-gown and choking ha-bloody-ha on cigarette smoke.

'I was wondering, Mr Bennett, if you've read any of the material I've given your wife.'

He blinked and adjusted his focus. 'Well, no, I haven't. Actually, I've got my own church. I'm Presbyterian. I don't have time to —' But the word *church* had extended his hearing and he suddenly realised that his sad little excuse was being exposed all over town. They were ringing everywhere, big bells, little bells, tattle tongues all, tintinabulation — poetically speaking. he was being judged by dozens of blasted church bells.

Ah, Miss Drainwater, you are an exceedingly clever woman. Like the professional thief you choose your moment well.

She was smiling at him but her expression was too simple, too open for triumph. She unfastened her bag and he caught a whiff of old perfume, the smell of every woman's handbag, as she fumbled in its depths for her books. 'Mr Bennett, as a concerned parent, you might be interested in one of these articles about aggressive tendencies in the young.' She was quoting now and her voice was strong. 'I'm sure all people are worried about the young people today who seem to be involved with drugs and violence at an increasingly early age. Where will it end? we ask ourselves. The answers are in the scriptures, Mr Bennett. As this article points out, we can hardly blame our children. In the last days the forces of evil will be let loose on the earth. Families will be divided and nations will rise against themselves.'

'I haven't got money with me,' he said. 'If you go back to the house —'

'I can get the money next time.' She was flicking pages. 'God has prophesied in his book of Revelation, "Babylon has fallen and become the habitation of devils and the hold of every foul spirit." This means that our children have to face all sorts of appalling abominations. It's a very disturbing thought, isn't it?'

He wanted to scratch himself. When I go back there I'll shoot the lot of them, he thought, and I shall bury Hazel in the garden with a tomato stake through her miserable heart. He felt depressed. The sun on his woollen shirt had started trickles of sweat which itched under his arms and on his chest like colonies of ants. If the world was going to end it had better get a move on.

When he thought about it, he had to admit it wasn't so much the itch that made him miserable as his inability to scratch in front of this — this Dullwater, Drainwater. He looked down at her shoes, mere scraps of nothing, then at his own size ten boots encased in wads of mud, and he was amazed at the extent of his cowardice. She went on about earthquakes, blood from heaven and falling stars. He didn't stop her. He gently scraped his boots on the top of his spade and let her talk while the sweat ran inside his corduroys and the bumble bees growled in the rows of broad bean flowers behind him.

'God is going to make all things new,' she said. 'He that

50

overcomes shall inherit everything, but the others, those not written in the Book of Life, they'll be cast into the pit of fire.'

He rubbed the back of his neck. The trench he'd dug was dusted with a mixture of superphosphate and blood and bone, and the seed potatoes, hardened to greenness, were in line to the half-way mark where he stood. 'Okay. Well. I'll take a copy. I don't want to rush you at all but — you know, I do have to finish this.'

'There's another short article on page twenty-six.'

'No. Look, I'm sorry but there's a lot to be done, Miss — Miss —'

'Gilwater,' she said. 'It's Mrs, Mrs Gilwater.' And her voice was thin again, so translucent that he saw clear through to the pink hair-ribbons and long, white socks. Curiosity stilled him. What kind of marriage could make a woman lose all the years between nine and forty? he wondered as he studied her face. Her mouth was small, you would call it undeveloped, but it wasn't an embittered mouth. Her grey eyes were round, clear and entirely without knowledge.

'You have children?' he asked.

She smiled. 'We haven't been blessed that way.'

'And your husband — he's still alive?'

She hesitated long enough for him to think, ah, so that's it, that explains it all, then she said, 'Oh yes. My husband is very well, thank you.'

'So you're both involved in this. I mean, does he do this kind of work with you?'

'I'm afraid not, Mr Bennet. My husband is not one of us yet. But he will be. The time will come, I know it. It must come. In the meantime he's in God's care and I pray for him every day.'

Her smile had the chill of total conviction and her voice, it was fine, all right, as fine as piano wire, cut him to the extent that he was defending himself when he said, 'What about your husband's attitudes? Don't they count?'

'They will change,' she said. 'He's a good man, my husband,

51

and many a good man has fallen prey to a Jezebel. He'll come back.

'When the scales fall from his eyes he'll leave her and come back to me and God's mercy. Seven years seems a long time but it's not long in God's reckoning. Jacob waited twice that for Rachel, and so will I, Mr Bennett. Yes, he will be returned to me.' Her white-gloved hand tapped between her breasts. 'I know it here for certain.'

He shut his mouth and thought, well now, that would teach him to mind his own business.

'It's a period of testing,' she said. 'There are women in the world, messengers of Satan in disguise, who make a career of destroying marriage and the Lord has permitted us to be brought to trial, praise his name. I consider it an honour, Mr Bennett, that God thought my marriage good enough for such a test.'

'And what if it isn't?' he said.

'I know it is. I know because God has given us his word, he does not try us beyond our limits.'

She was gesticulating with her books as though they were a handful of aces. Her eyes were bright with victory. He turned slightly so that he wouldn't have to look at her, and wondered what happened to women like this. Poor old Stormwater. She was too ignorant for heaven, too innocent for hell, and the odds were against her ever attaining either.

'Yeah, maybe so,' he said. 'I hope it works out.' He turned to her. 'Would you like a lettuce?'

'Oh.' Her smile wavered and she didn't seem to know. 'Only if — are you sure you've got one to spare?'

'Look at them.' He pointed to a row, spring-green and every plant fat-hearted.

'Oh yes. I see. Thank you, that would be nice.' She walked across the wet earth, at each step sinking the depth of her heel. 'I don't have a garden. It's just a room over a shop. I suppose, though, I could have a window box and grow a few herbs like parsley and sage. I wonder if parsley would be affected by diesel fumes? There's a bus stop outside, you know, underneath the window. Some days I have to keep the window closed.' She stopped by the lettuces. 'Aren't these awfully early?'

He crossed the garden and stood next to her. 'It's an early season,' he said, looking down on her hair which really wasn't too bad, good colour and nice, clean smell. 'Everything's come away like wildfire,' he said.

He unfolded his pocket knife and bent over the row, feeling the leaves for the most solid heart. He cut it and held it out to her but she was unprepared for the weight of it and she let it drop on the ground between them. They both reached out, leaning forward at the same time. Her arm brushed against his, a quick live touch, and she drew back so abruptly that she lost her balance and would have fallen had he not grabbed her hand. She gasped as though she had gone under cold water and tried to pull away but he tightened his grip on her wrist and held on for longer than was necessary. The glove made her hand feel like a small animal, smooth pelt over bones made hard with alarm.

'It's these shoes,' she said. 'The others are being repaired. The heels, see? I shouldn't have put them on this morning. See, how silly? Quite ridiculous.'

As he let her go, he thought, well, well, it's still there, all right, it's still very much there. Not so much of the lost soul after all. He gave her a long, considering look and she turned away in panic. 'Did I break that — that plant? Yes, I have. I'm so sorry, I should be more careful.'

'Don't worry,' he said.

'I'm afraid I'm very clumsy. I've always been clumsy. I hope it's not one of your more important plants.'

He shook his head and thought that, later, when he had time to expand the allegory, he'd be able to make a parable from the crushed tomato seedling, a sermon for Miss Rosewater. You mean you don't recognise this bit of green? It's broken and it will die. All things are meant to die, Miss Rosewater. Come, come, spend your time with the living.

'No,' he said. 'It's not important.'

Her cheeks were flushed and she was uncomfortable to the point of tears. 'I'd better let you get on with your work.'

He wanted to give her some sort of reassurance, but she was ready to leave and it would have been cruel to try and stop her.

'Your lettuce,' he said and bowed.

'Thank you very much.' She took the lettuce under her arm and started down the path but after a few steps she turned and although she was still pink with embarrassment she was able to look him in the eye. She moved her free hand in a small wave. 'Goodbye, Mr Bennett.'

He waved back. 'God loves you, Miss Rosewater,' he said.

His words came as a complete surprise to him. He stood facing her, unable to tell her what he'd meant. She was silent and waiting, her smile fluttering on and off, but he had nothing more to say to her.

What was there to say?

She went round the side of the house and he returned to his potatoes.

A few moments later Hazel came out of the kitchen. She'd got dressed and combed her hair round her shoulders.

'You're a fine one,' he said. 'I could have wrung your neck.'

She didn't answer. She walked round the garden, arms folded, inspecting the green rows, then she came back to him and said, 'You didn't buy one of her magazines.'

He stood up straight. 'No, by George, I didn't! I told her I would and then she went away with it.' He laughed. 'How did I get off the hook?'

Hazel wasn't laughing. She moved up close, put her arms round his neck and deliberately leaned against him.

Her perception appalled him. 'What do you think you're doing?'

She grinned then, and kissed him on the neck, but her eyes were still as watchful as a cat's. 'What did that woman take with her?' she said.

'A lettuce. I gave her a lettuce. Do you have any objection?'

'No, none at all.' She rested her face on the front of his shirt. 'You know something? You stink.'

'All right, all right.' He put his arms round her and asked, 'What are the boys doing?'

'Tearing the house apart.'

He turned her by the shoulders and steered her towards the path. 'Let's have a look in the shed,' he said.

# The Colonel and
# South America

In this house between night and day, the air of the Andes is marvellously clear and trembling with a light that seems to belong to another planet. The sky above the city of La Paz is rimmed with a rose colour. Snow-covered peaks on the horizon are pink, creased with mauve.

Along the Avenida 16 de Julio the buildings wear the same film of light like a membrane. Blocks of stone are softened by it, wrought-iron balconies are made exquisitely fragile. In the middle of the avenue the grey monument to Bolivar touches the eye with the texture of velvet.

There is no warmth to the morning. For all its promises the sun has not yet appeared and the temperature is close to freezing point. Local women in striped shawls and bowler hats hurry along the street trailing breath smoke. Some of the men are bent under large bundles of firewood or baskets of vegetables, but they, too, move at a shuffling run.

We stamp our feet at the edge of the road and blow against our hands. We turn in circles, tripping against our luggage and each other, our eyes spill water, our cheeks and noses are red. We sniff like a company of mourners.

The retired army colonel from Illinois raises his wrist to eye level. 'It's a quarter after the hour,' he says. 'Seven fifteen, know that?'

Everyone knows, no one answers. Amongst the group of French skiers, those nearest the Colonel exchange looks and try to move. The old man turns on them, hitting his knuckles together. 'You folk, you've only been here a few days, haven't you? Wait till you've had a month of it. You'll understand what I'm talking about.'

Next to me, a girl with red hair smiles and says through her teeth, 'Here we go again.'

'Get used to it right now,' says the Colonel. 'Sure as hell, you'll find it everywhere. Doesn't matter if it's a bus or a train or a plane. All these weeks Katie and I haven't gotten out of one place on time. Right, Katie?'

His wife smiles and nods. She has skin like a dried apple but her eyes are very wide and blue and seem no more than three years old.

The Colonel's breath hangs over the French skiers, the only passengers amongst us dressed against the cold. They sit on their suitcases and backpacks, thick in padded nylon windbreakers and snow-proof pants, ponchos, boots, mittens. Their faces, framed in wool or fur, are turned towards the Colonel with the polite smiles of the deaf.

'Don't count on leaving here before midday,' he says. 'No explanations. It just doesn't turn up. You stand around and stand around and then you march down to that bus office. Know what they tell you? Mucho sorry, bus broke down but there's another one on the way. It'll come in five minutes, they tell you. So you wait five minutes. You wait an hour. Then you go back wanting to know what the hell. They don't understand you. Those same guys, they talked to you in English an hour before. Now suddenly, no comprende your lingo. It's true. It happened to me and Katie in Caracas.'

The red-headed girl leans against her boyfriend. 'Hey, he's really something else.'

The boy whispers through her hair and puts his arms round her.

'We've gotten to take civilisation for granted, that's our trouble,' says the Colonel, clapping his fists together. 'The inefficiency in these countries is way beyond the comprehension of the average United States citizen. There's no sense of time or order. As for honesty, that old whatsamecallit could fossick with his lantern for a thousand years on this continent. The cab drivers now, take the cab drivers. Back home they might get a bit mouthy but they're honest. They're not out to rob you. You mademoiselles, you watch out. Don't ever let them see your pocket-books.'

'Is he going all the way to Cuzco?' says the red-headed girl.

'I think so.' The boys stands on his toes to see the labels of the Colonel's baggage. 'Yeah, Cuzco.'

The girl sucks in her breath. 'My God, twenty-four hours of it!'

She gets a sympathetic smile from three German women who look so alike they must be closely related. All are heavily built, have straight grey hair and pink faces with colourless eyebrows and lashes. The shortest and fattest of the three moves a step towards the girl and says, 'I think he is old for such a journey. Seventy-five, I think. Seventy-eight. It is not good for his bones, this cold air. When the bus comes he will be better.'

The boy looks at her, looks away again. 'Yeah,' he says. 'Sure.'

The girl says nothing.

'For us the cold is good,' says the German woman. 'We live in the mountains. Our blood is thick.'

The boy moves his eyebrows and laughs. 'You mean you enjoy this? Aw, come on —'

'Nein, nein, it is cold. We are all feeling with cold. But that poor man is more, I think. He has a look about him, my sisters tell me. They know. They are nurses.' She smiles. 'I am a teacher of mathematics.'

The boy unwraps his arms from the girl and reaches across to shake hands. 'Hi. We're Ken and Sandy from Escondido, California.'

'We've got the thinnest blood in the world,' says the girl.

The French skiers have moved, leaving the Colonel standing with his wife and three suitcases in a small square of chill sunlight. He stares after the group, his mouth open as though he is trying to remember something. His identity is stencilled across his bags but if it weren't, we would still guess him to be an army officer. His movements are precise, his back as straight as a gun barrel.

His wife opens a suitcase and takes out an alpaca rug, one of those circular things made from patches of brown and white fur. She wants him to wear it over his shoulders. He pushes it away. She insists.

'No, Katie, no. I said, don't fuss.'

Her reply is inaudible. She stands on her toes and tries to drape it round him.

'Katie, I'm not cold, dammit!'

She won't give in. He snatches the rug from her and wraps it round himself so that it stands out from his body in a cone. It changes him. He is now quite magnificent, like a figure from an Indian myth, tall, regal, a pre-Incan bird-man. Above the fur the face has a predatory look, eyes bold and quick-blinking, silver hair standing on end as though it is growing towards the sun. He uncovers his wrist. 'Know what the time is?' he says.

Along the avenue the morning traffic has increased greatly both in volume and noise. Local buses, overflowing with workers, hurtle down the hills to challenge each other at intersections with loud horns and brakes. About a hundred yards from us, a pointsman on duty moves as nimbly as a bull-fighter.

'Ach, those buses,' laughs the mathematics teacher. 'On Monday was no floor, just holes — you know, big holes under our seats for the stones and dust. So much dust! Our faces are all over powder — like clowns.'

'Yeah, well I hope we're not making it to Cuzco in one of those,' says Ken.

Sandy pulls away from him. 'Ken, I wouldn't. I'd rather go by train.'

'Okay, okay,' he says.

Our bus arrives at a time when no one is watching for it and it is, thank goodness, nothing like the local transport. Neither is it the luxury coach advertised in the tour brochures. There is no heating, windows are cracked, the 'Bar and WC' are a couple of crates of Fanta and a small cupboard with a door that will not close; but these things are unimportant. The vehicle is reasonably modern and has an engine that burns quietly, cleanly. All the tyres have adequate tread. Inside, the seats are comfortable.

Half a dozen Latin American passengers are already on board and settled for the journey. In the front seats beside the driver are two men in khaki overalls, presumably relief drivers. They get out to load the luggage on the roof of the bus.

The Colonel and his wife stay outside until last, guarding their suitcases. When all the other bags have been loaded, the Colonel allows one of the men to pass their three cases to his companions on the roof. The men don't understand English but there is more than enough meaning in the Colonel's tone to make them careful. The suitcases have to be resited on the luggage rack several times before the old man is satisfied.

Inside the bus, we can all hear the Colonel's voice. One of the Latin passengers says something in Spanish to the driver who looks out his side window at the Colonel, shrugs, spreads his hands palm downwards and rocks them from side to side. He and the passenger laugh.

I am seated next to a Peruvian mining engineer, a Senor Eduardo Lorenzo who is travelling back home to Puno. He has a quiet voice and the saddest eyes I have ever seen. When he laughs, the thin points of his moustache tremble and his face folds into a mask of grief. 'Always we have a crazy one,' he says. 'Make the travel interesting, no?'

The German women occupy three of the four spaces in front of me, the couple from California are further back on the opposite side. Sandy waves to attract my attention, then points to the two empty seats across the aisle from mine. She nods in the direction of the Colonel and draws her finger across her throat in a gesture of sympathy.

The Colonel is no longer in a hurry to leave La Paz. He comes slowly up the steps of the bus, trailing the alpaca cape from his shoulders. At the top of the aisle he stops and looks deliberately at each seat as though he is counting the passengers.

The man at the wheel makes impatient, winding movements with his hands. '*Ay Senor?*' he calls. '*Alli, alli!* '

'Ah-yee yourself,' says the Colonel without turning round. Still standing in the aisle, he takes off the rug and tries to fold it. His hands are quick but clumsy, his fingers arthritic, and the fur will not crease in neat lines. We wait, the engine running. The driver taps on the steering wheel. Finally the Colonel says, 'Here, you do it,' and passes the rug to his wife. He sits down by the window, she moves in beside him, but instead of folding the rug, she spreads it across their knees, tucking it in each side of the seat. For a moment he looks as though he's going to throw it off, then he smiles and says, 'That's nice, Katie. That's real nice.'

As the bus crawls out of the traffic, the German mathematics teacher turns round, half out of her seat, to see the passengers at the back. She says to us, 'The little French girl in the white hat, you know, her head hurts very bad. The girl from Lyon? She has the altitude sickness, poor child. The other ones tell me yesterday they go skiing at Chacaltaya, for all of the day from the morning to the dark.'

The man from Puno sighs disbelievingly. '*Mas alto!* '

'That is what I say to them.' The woman leans further over the seat. 'It is more than five thousand metres up high, that snow. I know mountains. I was born in mountains. But you tell me, who goes skiing with the angels, huh?'

'*Demasiado*,' says the man from Puno. 'Too much.'

The woman looks again towards the back of the bus and clicks her tongue. 'Ach, her face is as white as her hat, white as death, poor girl. She shuts her eyes.'

'Is no problem to — to breathe?' The man inhales deeply, one hand on his chest.

'*Nein*, her breaths is good, I think. It is the head with the pain — *como se dice?*'

'*Dolor de cabeza?*'

'*Ja ja, si*, a very big *dolor*, and I am thinking not so big *cabeza* to go skiing where no air is for her blood. When the blood is thin, do not hurry, do not go quick. It is bad, the gymnastic.' She glances at the Colonel and lowers her voice to hoarseness. 'That man, he is better now. He is warm and look at him, no troubles in the world.'

The Colonel rests back in his seat, dozing, his eyes almost closed, his head hanging forward, chin rocking gently against his collar. His wife is filing her fingernails.

The German woman's sister, one of the nurses, points to something out the window and the woman sits down heavily, clucking with surprise. From the back their heads look identical, grey hair cut short, red-rimmed ears. The third sister is a little taller and wears spectacles, but she too is a mixture of pink and grey.

The relief drivers are sitting beside the man at the wheel, talking to him between mouthfuls of biscuit. Their voices are shrill and their laughter sprays crumbs over their overalls and his. He smiles, nods but doesn't say much. He is very young. There is a fringe of oily black hair round his denim cap and he has a pock-marked skin. He drives slowly, too carefully if anything, heedless of the horn blasts behind him. It takes him more than an hour to get out of the La Paz basin and on to the straight, flat road of the altiplano.

The sun is now well up in the sky, whirling itself to splinters on the scratched windows. Where it falls across our laps there is warmth, but our voices still steam and most of us complain of numb feet. I envy the sleeping Colonel his fur rug.

But at least we are protected from the wind, not like the campensinos who travel together huddled in the backs of open trucks. On either side of the road the tussock is swept flat and the earth moves past us in spirals of brown dust. Everything has the colour of dust, the vegetation, animals, adobe houses, children, everything except the sky and the distant peaks which shimmer over the drabness with a kind of spiritual intensity.

A small boy holding a stick in one hand leans forward, face down and hugs his ragged poncho against his body. He is trying to drive a small herd of animals, a burro, a goat and two llamas whose long hair is parted by the wind. Ahead of him, a woman stares at the bus, one hand on top of her bowler hat, the other shading her eyes. Her skirt and shawl flap about her like empty sails.

'*Mucho viente*,' says the mining engineer. 'Is the time of the year, the wind is strong.' He smiles with a great sadness and says that if the wind is too strong, we might not get across Lake Titicaca for the waves. The barges are not big, he tells me. Last year in a high wind a bus went into the water, and the baggage claims are still not settled.

I ask him, 'What happens if we can't cross?'

He shrugs. 'We wait for the wind to go away.'

'How long does that take?'

'*Quien sabe*? Two hours — two days.' He shakes his head quickly. 'Is no problem to us now. We are many kilometres from the lake, and the wind changes all the time. We do not know until we come to Tiquina.'

A few minutes later we see the shores of Titicaca, ruffled blue water separated from the bare earth by clumps of reeds and the occasional fishing boat. Passengers get out of seats and open windows to take photographs, and almost at once the bus is full of cold air which swirls dust and debris in our faces.

The Colonel sits up straight, blinks and is fully alert, reaching for his camera. He pushes the rug from his knees and half-stands against the window, the instamatic pressed to his face. Click,

click. He steadies himself. Click. 'Think I got it, Katie. One of those boats like a pea-pod. Did you see it back there?' He sits down and wipes the lens with his handkerchief. 'You don't take snapshots?' he says.

She doesn't answer.

He leans forward. 'I said, I notice you're not taking any snapshots.'

He is talking to me.

'I'm sorry. No. No, I'm not much of a photographer.'

'Hey!' he says. 'You're English. Now how about that.'

'Actually, I'm a New Zealander.'

'No kidding? Katie, did you hear? We got a little lady all the way from New Zealand, Australia.'

'Not Australia,' I laugh. 'New Zealand is a separate country.'

'Yeah, well sure, I know that.'

'Not many people do.'

'Oh, we know about New Zealand. We've got friends who've been there three times and we've seen all their movies. You've got a real beautiful country down there, they tell me. What are you doing in this part of the world? Business trip or vacation? Say, you're not travelling alone, are you?'

'Yes.'

'Just on your own? Gee, I'm surprised they didn't warn you before you left home.'

'Warn me about what?'

'It's dangerous,' he says. 'That's what. Dammit to hell, it's dangerous enough for a man, and pardon my language, but a woman? How long you been here? Just a few days, huh? Believed everything they told you in the travel books. White-wash, that's all it is, little lady; hokum-pokum sales talk. Not one of those travel agents tell you what this God-forsaken continent is really like.'

'I wouldn't call it God-forsaken. That's one thing I wouldn't call it.'

'You a missionary or something?'

'No.'

'I reckon you got to be a missionary, totally dedicated, to survive in this place.'

I lean back in the seat. 'I think our experiences have been different.'

But he bends further forward until he is almost across his wife's lap. He points at me with a hooked finger. 'You just pray, little lady, pray you don't have an experience like ours.'

The mathematics teacher turns to him and says, 'Last Monday we have seen two missionaries from the United States. In a very little village, two boys who are looking so young and happy. They are here two years with work for their church.'

'They'll be Mormons,' says the Colonel.

'They are happy, those boys. They live in little houses with the peasants, but always, they tell me, it is important to boil the water — three-minute boil for the organisms.'

'I got nothing against missionaries,' says the Colonel. 'They're fine folk, the Mormons. That's what I mean when I talk about dedication. like some of the poor priests you see out here, working themselves into an early grave — for what? I mean, what can they hope to achieve apart from their own slice of pie in the sky? Corruption here is an institution a lot older and stronger than Christianity, I tell you.'

He is leaning towards the teacher and hitting his fist in the palm of his hand so fiercely that she blinks every time he makes a point. His wife, who is still carefully filing her nails, smiles and nods as he begins an account of the history of the Jesuits in Bolivia.

I glance at the mining engineer, but his face is turned away towards the window.

'The worst thing they ever did was kick the Jesuits out,' says the Colonel. 'Wouldn't you say so, Katie?'

She gives him a long and considering look, then blows the dust from her thumbnail. Her eyes are quite astonishing, whites unblemished by age or illness, the irises a clear blue and totally lacking in depth. Her gaze has an empty look like that of a waking child, yet she is not mentally unbalanced, at least not in any obvious way. She seems both relaxed and confident, her smile is not forced. Yet the smile, like the eyes, is without focus.

'The Latins have never gotten themselves assimilated,' says the Colonel. 'They still see themselves as Europeans living in another country. That's part of their trouble.'

The straight road has shrunk to a one-way track which winds in loops round the shore of the lake, and the bus is crawling over ruts in a slow, screaming gear. We drop into holes, lurch out of them again, meet clouds of dust on the corners and, too often for comfort, stop bonnet to bonnet in front of loaded trucks. There are no posts or fences to mark the side of the road. It drops steeply to the lake a hundred feet below. Above us, every square foot of the brown hills is terraced and cultivated, waiting for rain.

'The Indians'll never change,' says the Colonel. 'Four hundred years hasn't made the slightest impression except to add drink to their drug problem. The ones I was telling you about, you know, once every five years those villages have a duel to death? Sure thing, they do. The fittest young man from one village fights the fittest young man from the other village. With whips. They have these whips with tomahawks on the end. And then the village of the one who's the winner takes all the virgins of the defeated village.'

'Nein,' says the teacher. 'It is not true.'

'I tell you it is,' says the Colonel. 'It's the gospel truth.'

I look in question at the mining engineer.

'*Si*,' he says.

'You know what the life expectancy here is?' says the Colonel. 'Forty-five for men and forty-seven for women. Back in the States, forty-five isn't even middle-aged. Life begins at forty.' He scratches the end of his nose. 'They only have fights every five years, I'm told. That's how long it takes to get a new crop of virgins.'

The teacher laughs. 'I think you make a joke.'

'No, no. God's honour,' says the Colonel.

At the back of the bus one of the French boys is playing a guitar, holding the instrument vertically on his knees like a small 'cello and singing directly against the fingered frets. The song is lively, a French version of 'Old McDonald Had A Farm' and other members of the team shout out the animal sounds, breaking into laughter and wild cheering every time a wheel hits a pothole. They seem to have forgotten the girl in the white hat who lies face down across two seats, her hands over her head.

'You know how many revolutions they've had in this country?' says the Colonel. 'A hundred and seventy-nine.'

His wife sees something outside that draws her attention, and she sits on the edge of the seat, her eyes suddenly quick with interest. 'Where's the camera, Arthur?' She shakes his arm. 'Hurry up, get a shot of the children.'

We are coming down a hill to a village of adobe, thatch and white-washed stone, about twenty houses on either side of a narrow street, a church with a bell tower and a school. In the school grounds little girls in white aprons jump up and down, waving their arms over their heads at us. The real pleasure in their smiles affects everyone on board, and we wave back as though we have known them all our lives.

The Colonel has his head out the window. '*Buenos deeee-as!*'

'Did you get them?' asks his wife.

'Yep, I surely did. Aren't they darlings?'

A few barking dogs chase us from the village and half-way up the hill on the other side, before they're beaten back by distance and the wind. We are driving parallel to a row of skinny eucalyptus trees that are swept back and forth to breaking point, exploding fragments of leaves and twigs above us. Debris spins against the windscreen and small branches crackle under the wheels with a noise like fire. The driver slows the bus to walking speed.

At the top of the next hill, on a spur high above the lake, we are hit by the full force of the wind. The bus shudders and is slapped sideways towards the bank by a great air current which whistles through the cracks in the windows like some disaster warning. Below us, white-ridged waves race one behind the other along the length of the lake.

The man from Puno sighs and shakes his head.

'You all got your seasick pills?' laughs the Colonel to the German women.

When we arrive at Tiquina it's apparent to everyone that the bus cannot be ferried across the narrow neck of the lake. The wooden barge, which would no doubt be adequate on a calm day, rocks against the shore as frail as a toy against that back-ground of heaving blue and white water. The driver brakes near the edge and leans forward, chin on hands, staring morosely into the distance, while his two companions offer a rapid flow of advice. Amongst the passengers there is a bit of muttering but most of us are quiet, weighted into silence by helplessness.

After some minutes the driver makes an announcement in Spanish that is translated into English, then French, by one of the Latin passengers. There can be no crossing for the bus today, too much waves, too much wind. The barge will turn over.

'What do we do? Head back to La Paz?' says the Colonel.

The driver hears *La Paz* and shakes his head energetically.

'Please,' says his interpreter. 'All the passengers waits four hours. In four hours the bus from Cuzco reach the other side. See? Over there. We changes. The passengers goes across the lake in boats, the buses stays.'

'Is that what *he's* telling you?' The Colonel points to the driver.

'*Si, si*, we waits for the Cuzco bus.' The man repeats the full message in French and at the back of the bus there is an outbreak of groans and catcalls.

The Colonel looks at the French team and laughs. 'See, I told them. Back there in La Paz, I told them and they didn't believe me.'

The two relief drivers get out to talk to a man on the foreshore. Some of the French boys also go outside to stretch their legs and inspect the long row of fishing boats that move on their ropes like restless horses.

It is the hour of the siesta and Tiquina is almost deserted. In the streets only the dogs are busy, fighting or following their noses through trails of garbage. A man lies on his back on a stone bench, his poncho folded about him; another sits against a wall asleep in a foetal position. Away from the lake, the hillsides are marked with adobe houses which seem to have grown out of the earth like worm casts, the same colour as the terraced fields.

The air is harsh with sun and wind.

The relief drivers come back and begin unloading the luggage from the roof-racks, helped by the French boys. The man at the wheel gives a drum roll of instruction to the Latin passengers and again our interpreter stands up. 'Please, all the passengers waits now on the other side. The boat is ready. It go two times, one half in one time, the other half for the two time. We takes our baggage with us. The drivers goes to watch for our baggage is safe. This driver, he stay here. He go over when the bus from Cuzco come. You understands?'

The Colonel gets to his feet. 'Don't move, Katie. I'm going to get our bags.'

But the teacher is blocking the aisle, bent forward to see out the windscreen. 'God in heaven! We are going in *that* boat? In that water? Look at me, you think I am made for such little boats?' She turns to the Colonel. 'I don't swim so good, you know. Maybe I float — like a whale, huh?'

'You don't have to go now,' says the Colonel. 'We're not. I'm bringing our baggage in and we'll sit right where we are. When the other bus arrives, we'll go across with the driver.' He turns to me. 'You stay as well. You're better off with us. Over here, at least you can get back to La Paz. That bus from Cuzco, how do you know it'll turn up? You could get stranded.'

The teacher laughs. 'So? It is exciting. We are all of us having an adventure to tell when we get home.'

'We're not hankering after adventure,' he says.

She is serious. '*Ja*, I know, I was making the joke about the boat. There is no worry. It is good for everybody we all go when the man tells us.'

The Colonel's wife had been looking from one to another with a slightly bewildered smile. 'We're not going,' she says. 'We're staying here.'

The rest of us stand shivering by the edge of the lake as the boat is manoeuvred into position for the first load of people. A rough wooden plank which makes a gangway from the gunwhale to the shore, shifts constantly with the ebb and flow, and the two relief drivers have to stand waist-deep in water to hold the passengers as they board. A group of Latins go first, then five of the French team, then the three German sisters helping the girl who has the headache. I'm about to follow when the boatman yells, '*No mas!*' I step back quickly and the plank is pulled to the shore. The outboard motor starts, throwing streamers of black smoke into the wind, and the boat moves slowly out, rocking at such an angle that spray is thrown over its occupants.

The Californians stand beside me, watching. Ken says:

*And who be ye, would cross Lochgyle*
*This dark and stormy water?*
*O I'm the Chief of Ulva's isle,*
*And this, Lord Ullin's daughter.*

'Shut up, Ken,' says Sandy.

*'Twas vain: the loud waves lashed the shore*
*Return or aid preventing:*
*The waters wild closed o'er his child —*

'Ken, you're not funny.' Then she turns to me. 'I was saying, this lake gives me the creeps. Don't you think there's something sinister about it? I don't mean the wind, it's the way the earth is bare right down to the water's edge, as though it's not water at all but some kind of poison. I'd just hate to fall in that.'

Ken says, 'Jacques Cousteau came up here with a diving team a few years ago. They were looking for archaeological findings but I don't think they found much. Mud was too thick. I read they had problems diving at this altitude. They had to change all their calculations for decompression. There was a doctor with them. He took blood samples because they all had bad headaches, and guess what, he found that each of them was short of about three million red corpuscles.'

'That's what's wrong with the girl,' says Sandy.

'Yeah,' says Ken. 'She looks sick.'

'Is she ever! I've never seen anyone so pale.'

'They said she was all right till yesterday when they went skiing. Even here, each time we breathe we get only half the oxygen we'd get at sea level.' He whistles softly for a while, digging his heel into the damp earth, then he looks out across the lake and clasps his hands together.

*Come back! Come back! he cried in grief*
*Across this stormy water:*
*And I'll forgive your Highland chief,*
*My daughter! Oh my daughter!*

The boat is nearly on the other side, visible only on the crests of the waves where we see it tipping like a see-saw. Near us, the man on the stone bench is still asleep. A woman fills two buckets from the lake and walks past us, smiling a greeting. With each step, water slops into her shoes.

The passenger who translated for the driver comes towards us, his shoulders hunched, his hands spread as though he is begging alms. 'The old man make a problem,' he says. 'He and his wife wishes to stay with the bus.'

'That's right,' I say. 'Until the bus from Cuzco arrives.'

'Is not possible. The driver want everybody out to lock the door, you understands? He want to visit his mother's brother in the village, but he can no leave his bus when the door is open. The old man wait here, is okay, okay, but no in the bus. He get out.'

'Have you told him?' I ask.

'*Si, si, pero es un vieje loco!*' The man taps his head. 'He understand nothing, senorita. Listen to him!'

We hear raised voices from the bus behind us.

'Please, senorita, you speaks to him. Tell him he and the wife gets out. Is important. Now.'

'I don't think he will, but if you like, I'll try.'

'You're dealing with senile paranoia,' says Ken. 'Pressure him and you'll only increase his fear. He won't budge an inch.'

'I no understand,' says the man. 'The driver, he wish to lock his bus.'

The Colonel is sitting in the aisle on top of their three suitcases. His face is mottled red and blue with anger, and he stabs his forefinger at the driver who shouts back in shrill and rapid Spanish. Katie is in her seat, watching as though from some great distance. When I enter, she stares at me for several seconds before giving a smile of recognition; but the Colonel's face brightens instantly; he stops in the middle of a threat to the driver and says with triumph, 'You're staying with us!'

I have no feeling for him and yet all the same there is a sense of guilt, of betrayal. 'No, I'm going across now. Don't you think you should come too?'

'I told you, I told him, we're not budging.'

'He wants to lock up. Apparently he can't go away unless he secures the bus.'

'Why should he?' says the Colonel. 'You know where he wants to go? Off to visit relatives. He's not paid for that. His first and foremost duty is to his passengers.'

'You're making things a bit awkward for him.'

'Not half as awkward as they're going to be if he lays a finger once more on our baggage. Listen, little lady, I admire your attitude, but it's not realistic. This is not Australia. For your own personal safety I'm telling you, stay here.'

'Why? The boat's safe enough. We watched it with the first load. Besides, if this wind continues, it's possible the waves will be higher in another four hours.'

'I wasn't talking about the waves.' His eyes hold a hard, questioning look. 'You think I'm a stupid, old fool talking through a hole in his head, right? Yep, you're like those French kids, just won't be told. Well, you come here a moment. No, closer. I'm going to show you something. Katie?'

His wife turns and gazes at him.

'Katie? Go on.'

With a small, apologetic smile, Katie raises her arms and scoops back the curls from either side of her face. The lobes of both ears have been mutilated. Half of one is missing, leaving a v-shaped edge red with suture marks, the other is deeply fissured by scar tissue.

'Take a good look,' says the Colonel. He calls to the Californian couple who've come into the bus behind me. 'You two, as well. Come over here and see what you get when you wander round these villages. That happened in Colombia — place only the size of this and in broad daylight, not three weeks ago. You see, do you? You see?'

Katie moves her head from side to side and says, 'They were after my earrings.'

Sandy averts her eyes and backs away, making a noise somewhere at the back of her throat.

'Man, that's awful!' says Ken.

'I bought her gold earrings in Bogota, hoops with little bells on them. They were kids, you know, only twelve or thirteen. Must have been a dozen of them. They knocked me down, got my watch and movie camera. Those things didn't matter. It was her. They kept pulling, you know, just pulling and pulling. I heard her screaming. I couldn't do anything. There were a whole lot of them on top of me, banging my head against the sidewalk. Bits of kids, no older than choirboys. They pulled those earrings right out of her ears.'

Katie lets her hair fall back in place. 'The doctors said they sometimes cut off people's fingers to get gold.'

Ken's face puckered with vicarious pain. 'Oh man,' he keeps saying. 'Man, that really is bad.'

'What gets me,' says the Colonel, 'is no one lifted a finger to help.'

Ken shakes his head. 'If that had happened to Sandy and me, I think we'd have gone straight back to California.'

'We tried to get home. We booked a flight the next day, direct route Bogota to Miami. Then we found out we couldn't get refunds on all our other bookings. Paid in advance, you see — tours, hotels, bus companies, guides. Sure, we could have gone back but we'd have lost about four thousand dollars. I tell you, son, we saved seven years for this vacation, and not once in that time did anyone tell us what the place was really like.'

The driver interrupts, shouting at the Colonel and waving his hands.

Ken says gently, 'The boat is back. He wants us all to get out.'

'If you still choose to go in spite of my warnings, then that's your affair,' says the Colonel.

The driver gets hysterical. '*Por favor, senor, el barco, el barco —*'

'Go to hell,' says the Colonel.

The crossing is not as bad as we feared. The boat is small but stable, an old navy lifeboat made of some heavy wood which rides through the water sluggishly, unaffected by the strong wind gusts, and although the outboard motor spews thick, black smoke and makes alarming noises when we lift over the crests of waves, it, too, seems to have a strong constitution. Ken and one of the French boys ride with their heads over the side, their eyes shut, but we reach the shore before either of them is actually sick.

The village looks much the same as the one we've left except for a building which resembles a medieval castle and is, we are told, the headquarters of the Bolivian Navy. Beyond it, the hills are almost a mirror image of the slopes on the other side, brown and bare and stepped in stone-walled terraces.

Most of the passengers are standing in the village plaza with loaves of bread and bottles of soda bought from one of the small shops. I buy a loaf, a slice of white cheese, and sit on the ground beside a wall, out of the wind, feeling the pressure of the sun on my eyelids.

Sandy and Ken flop down beside me and a short time later a young Indian girl, thirteen or fourteen, settles near us to feed her baby. '*Buenos tardes, senorita.*' She smiles at Sandy and joggles the child to make it suck.

Sandy passes a cigarette to Ken. 'You know, it was pretty dumb to wear gold earrings amongst impoverished peasants.'

'She wouldn't think, Sandy. They don't have that kind of social awareness.'

'Yeah, I guess so,' she says. 'It was a hell of a thing to happen to the poor old girl. God, those ears! No wonder she looks spaced out half the time. He's different. The hostile attitude he's got, with him it goes deeper than a mugging. That man is a prime example of irreconcilable culture shock. Could be why it happened to them. People like that, they tend to fulfil their own fears.'

'I agree with Fraulein whatsername,' says Ken. 'He's too old. He shouldn't have got any further than Florida.'

'You can't blame the kids,' says Sandy. 'They're the victims of a much greater injustice. The way we parade amongst these people showing off our material wealth — who do we think we are, huh? Of course they've got a right to steal. Everything's been stolen from them.'

'If I'd been in their shoes,' says Ken, 'I'd have flown home immediately and to hell with the four thousand dollars.'

'That partly illustrates my point, Ken. His generation is conditioned to automatically put money first.'

'I feel sorry for the driver,' says Ken.

'Yeah, me too,' she says.

I excuse myself and move as far as is tactfully possible away from their opinions. This day has been full of turbulence of one kind or another and I feel the need for solitude, for a place where I can spin some small web of calm round myself. I find it, a sheltered, sun-warm patch at the side of some steps behind a shop, and within minutes I'm dozing. Through the wall of the shop comes a babble of voices but they are in Indian dialect.

Aymara, I think. I don't know. It doesn't matter. Voices without meaningful language are not demanding, can in fact be as soothing as the noise of wind or water.

I am wakened by the Colonel's voice, distant but loud; that, and the cold of the late afternoon shadows. I stand up and walk stiffly to the plaza, wondering what all the shouting is about, not really caring. The bus from Cuzco is here. It's the same model as the one we left on the other side, and covered in dust. A crowd moves about it, and amongst the strangers who have just arrived, I see familiar faces pressing towards the door, anxious to board and get on with the journey. The Colonel is some twenty yards nearer the lake, with his wife, their baggage, and the driver with the pock-marked skin who sullenly stares at the ground.

'If I were a younger man, I'd punch your head in,' yells the Colonel.

The driver spits on the earth and tries to move away, but the Colonel grabs him by the front of his overalls and holds him at arm's length, shouting to anyone who will listen. 'He locked us in! Godammit, we were locked in that bus near three hours!'

Several of the passengers come forward, but it is Katie and the German teacher who persuade him to let the boy go.

The driver's head comes no higher than the Colonel's shoulder and their eyes do not meet until the boy has backed off several paces. He throws the Colonel a look of hate, brushes the front of his overalls and walks off, leaving the old man to cope with his bags.

'I tell you to come with us,' says the teacher, lifting one of the suitcases. 'We have a very good afternoon over here. We walk up on the hill to see the church — so beautiful, you know. Why you do not come, huh?'

'He did it out of sheer spite!' The Colonel trembles and saliva runs down his chin. 'That Indian, he locked the door from the outside.'

'He couldn't leave his bus unlocked,' I say.

'He wasn't supposed to leave it! I'm reporting him to the bus company the moment we get to Cuzco. He's going to lose his job over this, I promise him. He's supposed to stay with his bus — and his passengers.'

As we get ready to board, Ken says, 'Do you think he means it?'

'*Nein*,' whispers the German woman. 'Cuzco is tomorrow, tomorrow is different.'

The three drivers stay outside checking the last of the luggage, the engine, the tyres, while the passengers make themselves as comfortable as possible for the nineteen-hour journey ahead. One of the relief drivers gets in behind the wheel and starts the engine, while the other checks passengers against the company list. Finally the boy in the denim cap, still glowering, swings himself up the steps and sits beside the replacement driver.

The Colonel leans forward and bellows, 'I haven't finished with you!'

The boy turns his head away and the Colonel sits back muttering, 'He'll pay for that. Sure as hell, he's going to pay. Deliberate — it was a deliberate act. He knew there was no way we could open the door from the inside.'

We move from the shadows of the village and up the hill to the late-afternoon sunlight. 'There is the church,' says the German woman. 'In the inside it is so pretty. Claudette is with us also for the walk.' She looks back to the mining engineer. 'You know Claudette, the little girl in the white hat? Her head gets better. She drinks a medicine in the village and it is very good for the pain.'

I look up at the rear-vision mirror to see the French girl, but my view is blocked by Ken who comes down the aisle, his arms out to steady himself. He stops near me, leans against the side of the German woman's seat and says to the Colonel, 'You folks okay now?'

The Colonel stares at him, one eyebrow raised in a return question.

'I'm asking a favour,' says Ken. 'That business three weeks ago,

I appreciate how traumatic it must have been — for both of you. But man, it was in another country, with other people. For your own sakes, try not to let it affect you here. That driver wasn't being vindictive. He didn't know what else to do.'

The Colonel's face has set into an uncompromising system of straight lines, his eyes and mouth are small. 'You speaking to me, young man? Then have some manners. Get your hands out of your pockets and stand up straight.'

For a moment Ken doesn't move, then he takes his hands from his pockets and his cheeks turn a dark, angry red. We see his nostrils flare, the movement of muscles at the edges of his mouth, and we flinch in anticipation of the reply. It doesn't come. Instead the boy goes back down the aisle, almost in a stumbling run, and when I next look in the rear-vision mirror, he and Sandy are sitting with their heads together.

The wind hasn't lessened. Along the road, families straggle home with their laden burros or flocks of alpaca, both people and animals staggering against the gusts, heads down, eyes half-closed. We see a man crawling on the roof of his house, weighting down the sheets of iron with large stones. High on the hills, under the rocks, there are long, white seams of ice.

Ken comes to the front again, but this time he walks briskly, one-two-one-two, and stands to attention, military style, in front of the Colonel. Someone at the back of the bus laughs. Ken's eyes flicker and he almost grins as he salutes. 'Sir! Excuse me, sir!'

The Colonel looks up at him, surprised. Then slowly the tight lines of his mouth form curves and his entire face opens up into a smile as soft as that of a girl in love. 'Yes, son? What is it?'

Ken brings his hand down from the salute and glances towards the back of the bus. 'It doesn't matter,' he says, and returns to his seat.

# APPLE WINE

Ellen was looking for three perfect roses to go on the table. 'The storm has done almost no damage at all,' she said as she leaned over the bushes, her secateurs probing like the pincers of a large beetle. 'Which do you prefer, Hetty? Pink or white?'

But her sister was in the hall talking on the telephone to Muriel. 'I said the garden, dear.' Her voice came out the front door and rolled across the verandah, every word clear and the shape of a bell. 'We decided to have the reading out-of-doors today. Yes dear. Oh indeed yes. Quite superb. Ellen's put the wicker chairs under the walnut tree and there's plenty of shade, but I suggest you bring your panama. No dear, your hat. Do bring your hat.'

Ellen pulled a pink rose towards the secateurs and waited. Her sister often said things were quite superb. It was a figure of speech which described Hetty's vitality more than anything else, but today the expression was so rightly fitting it had taken on a new sound, magnificent, like a phrase from the hallelujah chorus. To Ellen's mind, there was no better way of describing the

79

transformation wrought by an overnight change in the weather. It was quite superb.

The lawn was still very damp, of course, but it had risen from the earth as thick as living fur, glistening, patched at the edges with the shadows of trees. And the roses, yesterday half-drowned, had inhaled the sun and expanded until they were almost bursting with colour and perfume.

Ellen touched the face of the pink rose and thought, angel skin, it was like blushing angel skin, then, hearing Hetty on the verandah, she called out, 'Do you remember what Daddy used to say about the rain? How it was the angels weeping for their sins?'

'Did he, dear?' said Hetty, shaking the white cloth over the table. 'No Ellen, those are too pale for the tea set. That red one, dear, growing by the thingummy — yes, yes, that's it.'

'I wonder if it was original,' said Ellen. 'Knowing Daddy, it probably was.'

Hetty didn't comment. She had changed the focus of her spectacles by lifting them away from her nose and was watching Ellen select the flowers. 'Muriel thinks it's time we had a chat to Olive,' she said.

Ellen carefully trimmed a stem. It was an old rose with single petals round yellow stamens and a heavy perfume unrefined by breeding. Too rich for the tea table, she thought.

'Did you hear me, dear? I believe at times you're as deaf as Muriel. I was talking about Olive. Muriel feels we've let it go far too long and the sooner we say something, the better for Olive's sake. Wouldn't you agree? Ellen? Ellen, are you listening?'

She closed the secateurs and brought the flowers over to Hetty. 'They're a nice colour,' she said. 'But I fear everything will smell of roses.'

'Muriel saw Stella last night. Stella says she can't come back to the reading group while Olive's in it.' Hetty flattened the creases in the cloth. 'We should do it today,' she said.

Ellen took the cut-crystal vase from the tea trolley and set it at the centre of the table with the three red roses leaning out from its rim. The light through the walnut tree lay in shivering shapes on the table, striking the vase so that its reflection on the cloth held splashes of white fire extending into rainbows and two red spots like wine stains.

She turned. 'Hetty, let's have a bottle of the apple wine.'

Her sister stopped mid-sentence as though someone had put in her mouth something to be tasted. She smiled. 'What a superb idea. Yes, indeed yes, a bottle of the good batch and we'll serve tea after the reading. Oh Ellen, you are a clever thing with flowers. It's so pretty —' She softly clapped her hands. 'We'll use the decanter,' she said.

It seemed rather frivolous to get out Daddy's decanter for their homemade apple wine and Ellen was surprised that Hetty had suggested it. As she opened the cabinet door she felt her father's disapproval in the stiffness of the hinges and she called to Hetty in the kitchen, 'We'll use the good glasses too, won't we?'

'Of course, dear!' Hetty shouted back and in a voice so reckless that Ellen laughed into the dark corners of the teak shelves.

Muriel came before they had finished setting the table, deliberately early so that she could talk about Olive. She was wearing a white and navy dress with a green silk scarf to hide the cord of her hearing machine, and a hat of yellowing straw. In a brown paperbag under her arm she carried the large-print edition of *Lorna Doone*. For some small time she stood by the verandah to fully admire the garden and exclaim over the stocks and lavender, geraniums, roses, the table under the tree, 'Gosh, Hetty, your apple wine. We are in for a treat.' Then she sat heavily in one of the wicker chairs and pulled off her gloves, finger by finger. 'I came in a taxi cab. Olive offered to bring me, which was jolly decent of her.' She looked at Hetty. 'She's been more than generous with her motor, I don't deny it.'

'We always pay for the benzine, dear,' said Hetty.

'The spirit of generosity,' said Muriel. 'We'll find it difficult to accept the loss of our little excursions, especially the concerts.

We'll miss the concert season. I say, Hetty, there must be someone in the village. Are you sure we haven't overlooked the possibility? What about that friend of yours related to the Scott-Turners, Mrs Calder? Doesn't she drive a motor car?'

'She had a stroke,' shouted Hetty.

'Pam Calder? Oh Hetty, what a shame. I am sorry to hear that. Well then — who else? Ellen, do you have an acquaintance with a motor?'

'I'm afraid I don't,' said Ellen.

'Pardon, dear?' said Muriel.

Hetty leaned over Muriel's chair. 'Ellen doesn't want to talk about it. She thinks we're being unfair. Unfair. To Olive. She thinks we're trying to put poor Olive out in the snow. Muriel, do switch on your deaf aid.'

'Unfair?' Muriel fumbled with the pocket on her bodice and her hearing machine whistled like an untuned wireless. 'Does she?' The noise stopped. 'Is that what you really think, Ellen?'

But Ellen didn't know what she thought, only that she believed no one had the right to turn a beautiful day to unpleasant purpose, so she nodded affirmation and sat in the opposite chair, leaning back until Muriel's head was barely visible above the table.

Muriel laughed. 'Olive, I imagine, will be vastly relieved. Of course she will, Ellen. Poor soul gets so fearfully bored with our fuddy-duddy ways, her only refuge lies in sleep or photos of her grandchildren. She'd have drifted away months ago if she didn't have our only means of private conveyance. Loyalty, Ellen. Loyal and generous to a fault, that's our Olive. Years ago Winkie had a batman cast in the same mould. The salt of the very earth.'

Ellen said nothing. The table rose between them like an altar with the white linen cloth, the decanter and glasses, the crimson roses already open to the stage of dropping. There was no sediment in the wine. It glowed in the decanter a pale gold colour but with a look of age to it, as though they had fermented pre-war sunshine in a vintage year. The long-stemmed glasses which had been covered with the fine dust of a locked cupboard were now so clean they looked as frail as soap bubbles.

And, as Ellen had predicted, everything smelled of roses.

'Our poor little group,' Hetty was saying. 'We've been disappearing like the ten little nigger boys. Do you remember, Muriel, the meeting at Cynthia's and how she used to read from that very odd lectern with the carved monkeys on it? Now Cynthia's gone. It was quite sad, dear, very sudden, in a nursing home in Auckland, I believe.'

A stillness came into the garden and a quiet which they held not so much for the passing of Cynthia who had, God bless her, been very trying at times, but for the resurrection of her drawing room and the afternoons they'd spent in it.

After a while Muriel sighed and said, 'I know, Hetty. You told me several times.'

'Did I, dear?' said Hetty. 'I don't remember.'

Olive came late and in a hurry. The moment they decided to pour the wine without her, they heard the little motor car crying out with the suddenness of its halt outside their hedge, and they put the stopper back in the decanter. They heard a car door slam and then immediately, another. Hetty and Muriel looked a question at Ellen who shook her head and stood up, trying to see through the trees. She sat down again quickly. 'I think she has brought a gentleman friend,' she said.

'A what?' said Muriel in a hushed tone, but it was clear from her expression of disbelief that she had heard and understood.

'Oh dear,' said Hetty, and she turned her chair so that her back was to the gate.

None of them got up to greet Olive. She bustled up the path, large in pink and lavender, with a young man following several paces behind her.

Very young, observed Ellen, very tall and so fair his hair caught the sun like thistledown.

He saw them first and said something to Olive, who turned at the point of knocking on the front door, and gave a cry of surprise. She came across the lawn with small quick steps, calling, 'Oh now! Oh my, I mean to say, isn't that just lovely? Isn't it beautiful? Like a scene from the movies, you know, with the garden in the background. Oh, I never in all my born days saw such a picture. You girls, you look just like royalty, don't they, Gareth?' She turned back to the young man. 'Girls, this is Gareth Malleson, my eldest grandson.' Then, taking him by the arm, she introduced him to each of them in turn.

He was only a boy, Ellen decided, tall and well-grown, but with a freshness to his complexion which indicated that a shaving brush was still new to him. He had blue eyes and straight fair hair which fell over his eyes when he leaned forward. His trouser was of a coarse cream fabric with buttoned pockets on the legs and he wore a pink and white striped shirt open at the throat. Round his neck hung a gold chain with some kind of coin or medal attached.

He was unusually polite for a young man of the day, and seemed well enough at ease. 'Nan's always talking about her reading group,' he said. 'I was glad for the opportunity to meet you.'

'Gareth's not staying,' said Olive, taking the empty chair. 'He's just dropped me off so he can borrow the car for the afternoon, haven't you, love?' She smiled up at him. 'He's picking me up again at five.'

He would have gone then, but Hetty, perhaps touched by his charming manner or her own initial coldness, held on to the arms of her chair and almost stood. 'Before you go, Mr Malleson, will you please join us in a glass of apple wine?'

'Thank you,' he said. 'Sure. I'd like to.'

'We have extra glasses,' said Hetty, 'and Ellen will get you a chair.'

But the young man insisted he'd rather sit on the ground, no, it wasn't all that damp and no, no, he wouldn't get grass stains, see, he'd make sure he didn't. He unfolded his handkerchief and spread it by the base of the walnut tree, then he came back to the table and offered to pour. 'It's my job,' he said. 'I'm a waiter.'

'Just listen to him,' laughed Olive. 'Of course he isn't a waiter. He's at university. He's going to be a lawyer. Don't let him kid you, girls, he's an awful tease.' And she smiled at him as though he were made of precious metal.

'It is my job,' he said. 'Two nights a week I pour wine and I'm very good at it. I should be. I've been a part-time wine waiter for nearly two years.' He took the stopper from the decanter and held it under his nose. 'Seventy-seven,' he said. 'A very good season for Granny Smiths.'

At that, even Muriel laughed and the sunlight fairly danced across the table.

Olive eased off her shoes and stretched her feet. 'I like a drop of cider now and then. It's got a kick like a mule if you over-indulge yourself, but a glass or two doesn't hurt.'

'This isn't cider, dear,' said Hetty. 'It's apple wine.'

'Oh?'

'They're very different,' said Hetty.

'Well go on, you could have fooled me,' said Olive.

The young man poured the pale wine into a glass, neatly twisting his wrist so that not a drop spilled on the tablecloth. His hands were yet at the bony stage, long fingers, large knuckles. 'What's the difference?' he asked.

'One can make cider of any apple,' said Hetty. 'Oh yes, indeed, any type, any quality. In fact if one leaves the apples to fall off the tree and rot in the grass of their own accord, they will make cider.'

'And wine?' he said. 'How do you go about making that?'

'We use only the best apples,' said Hetty. 'An equal quantity of dessert, cooking and crab apples. Then we add refined sugar. That's another of the essential differences between wine and cider. Cider has no added sugar. The process is the same as for any wine, Mr Mallieson, but there is much to go wrong — yeastiness, haze, rope, thinness, acidity. We find that only one year in four produces excellence. This is one of our better rackings.'

'It looks like a sylvaner riesling,' he said.

'Nothing so innocuous,' said Muriel. 'Hetty's apple wine is ambrosia and you'll need the stamina of the gods if you're going to drink it like your riesling.'

'It is — a substantial wine,' said Hetty.

He brought the glasses to them with the small niceties of presentation he'd use in his employment, heels together, a flourish from the waist that turned a stoop into a bow, then he took his own glass and sat with his back against the tree trunk. 'Your very good health,' he said.

'Cheers,' said Olive.

'Good health,' said Muriel.

The wine had only the faintest taste of apples, Ellen thought. Mostly it was flavoured with the season of the picking, the light chill of a mist, the crispness of a little frost and over it all, the warmth of the sun. She leaned back against the cushions to savour better the total effect of the beautifully balanced glass and its straw-coloured content.

'This is a fantastic wine!' the young man was saying. 'It's so smooth on the palate, so — so rounded.'

'Yes,' said Hetty. 'It's quite superb, isn't it?'

'Just goes to show you're never too old to learn something new,' said Olive.

'I assume you're on holiday,' said Hetty. 'From where, may I ask?'

'Christchurch,' he said. 'I don't get up this way often, not as often as Nan would like. I work most of my vacations and, well, you don't fly five hundred miles just for a weekend visit.'

Olive had her bag open on the arm of Muriel's chair. 'This is the daughter who lives in Christchurch, Edna my eldest, Gareth's mother. I showed you the other day, remember, taken outside their new home, all five of them, the two girls and Gareth standing there by his Dad.'

Ellen sipped in silence. The green shade was spotted and barred with sunlight which moved every time a breeze disturbed the tree so that they seemed to be in the flickering current at the bottom of some woodland pool, like a group of trout or grayling. She watched the shadows move across the young man's face and saw his hair float over his forehead as he nodded, listening.

I'm so glad I've got Hetty, thought Ellen suddenly. The warmth of the wine had made her feel sad for Muriel living on her own, no one to care for. Poor Muriel, her only daughter had married a dark gentleman from the Islands who had taken her away to live with his family, and Muriel had not seen her in twenty-seven years.

I don't know what I'd do without Hetty, Ellen thought. I've so much to be grateful for.

Muriel had taken the photograph from Olive and was holding it at arm's length towards the young man. 'I say, Hetty, he looks awfully like a young John Ridd.'

Hetty looked and slowly nodded.

'He does, doesn't he?' said Muriel in a deliberately teasing manner. 'What a coincidence. We have a visitation from the hero of this very novel!' And she patted the package in her lap. 'Look, Ellen, wouldn't you say he was none other than John Ridd in person?'

'No,' said Ellen. 'John Ridd was of much broader stature and he had a beard.'

'But I'm sure he didn't always have a beard, dear,' said Hetty, and their laughter surrounded the boy who blushed and put his head down, his composure gone.

Olive said, 'Don't worry, love. John Ridd's everybody's heart-throb. He's a big fellow built like an ox on the outside but a real kewpie doll underneath, kind, as cuddlesome as they come.'

The boy's face was pink and his eyes were down. He tried to say something with hand movements.

Muriel was enjoying herself. 'He gets — John Ridd gets most awfully intimidated by compliments.'

Hetty stopped laughing and turned her glass in her hands. 'Have you read *Lorna Doone*?' she asked him.

He shook his head.

'Oh what a pity,' said Hetty. 'It's a book best read in one's early years. Ellen selected it for the reading group because it was a favourite of her girlhood, but I think it's a mistake to revisit the places of one's youth. Wouldn't you agree? Everything seems so small and so ordinary when one goes back. With *Lorna Doone* one feels that all the best pages have been removed.'

'I don't,' said Ellen. 'I find the story as touching as ever. As for the descriptions of the English countryside, they're beautifully written and quite wasted on a child. I'm sure I didn't appreciate Mr Blackmore's penmanship nearly as much when I was young.'

'Oh yes, indeed yes,' said Hetty. 'He paints delightful little landscapes. But what about the romance, Ellen, that splendid passion between Lorna Doone and John Ridd — how improbable to the adult reader. At no time in the history of men and women since Adam, could friendship exist on such stilted utterances. It's so childish dear.'

Ellen smiled. Hetty, she thought, was getting a little tiddly.

Muriel had taken their large-print edition from its bag and was turning the pages. 'We missed an extraordinary thing, Hetty. Did I tell you? Going back, I discovered an unaccountable change in the character of Mrs Betty Muxworthy. Most extraordinary.' She looked at the boy. 'Betty Muxworthy is a domestic servant in the Ridd household.'

'An unpleasant woman,' said Hetty.

'Embittered by fortune,' said Muriel. 'Here it is. On page 49 when she first appears, she has a lilting Irish brogue. Listen to this: "Men is so desaving," she says, "and so is galanies; but the most desaving of all is books with their heads and tails, and the speckots in 'em lika peg as have taken the maisles. Some folks purtends to laugh and cry over them. God forgive them for liard!" But look here, a few pages further on and for the rest of the book, she has a broad Devon dialect: "Zailor, ees fai! ay and zarve un raight!" There, what do you make of that? Absolutely different.'

'Nothing,' said Hetty, waving her glass. 'He made a mistake, dear.'

'He didn't,' said Muriel.

'Oh, he did,' said Hetty. 'Mr Blackmore was not the most gifted of writers in the portrayal of character, but never mind, he was obviously a kindly man. The character of John Ridd assures us that.'

'Assures us what?' said Muriel whose hearing machine was whistling again.

'That he was kind,' shouted Hetty.

Already quite tiddly, thought Ellen, and in fine form. By evening she would have one of her heads.

'I see,' said Muriel, vaguely.

Ellen said, 'Hetty, how do you know John Ridd was an autobiographical portrait?'

'He was,' said Hetty. 'Indeed he was, my dear. When only one character in the book is real, one can be sure he's the author.' She held out her glass. 'Now our young John Ridd is going to help us to some more wine.'

Ellen didn't see what happened next. In standing to take Hetty's glass, the boy somehow knocked over his own. The noise of breaking crystal was loud and discordant as though someone had upset a harpsichord. Ellen heard it in every part of her body.

The boy sucked in his breath with a stricken sound and stood with his back to Ellen, looking at the fragments.

'Jolly bad luck,' said Muriel.

'It's not important,' said Hetty. 'Don't concern yourself.'

'It must have hit the root of the tree.' he said. 'I'm sorry, I didn't see it. I must have kicked — Jees, I'm sorry.'

Daddy's wineglass, mourned Ellen, rocking with pain. Oh, how awful. Daddy's beautiful glass.

'Don't give it a thought,' said Hetty.

Olive got out of her chair. 'Gareth, Gareth!' With her hands on her knees and her arms set like wings, she bent over, looking for the pieces in the grass by the tree. 'You're such a clumsy boy.

That was antique, you know, you can never replace it for love or money.'

'Olive, don't make a fuss,' said Hetty. 'There are five of us and we still have five glasses. Olive. Please. You'll cut your fingers.'

'I'm sorry,' said the boy. 'I know they're rare. I feel terrible.'

'All his life he's had two left feet,' said Olive.

'It just happened,' he said.

'No, no,' said Muriel. 'Not in your 'kerchief, that could be nasty.' She handed him the brown paperbag which had held the book. 'Put it in there and do be careful of the splinters. Oh, I say, cheer up, it's not the end of the silly old world. Bear in mind that John Ridd also had two left feet.'

'All of you leave the wretched thing,' said Hetty. 'Mr Malleson, put that down and we'll attend to it later. Come over here. You may pour us all some more wine, my dear.'

He stood up slowly and brushed his hair away from his forehead. 'Do you trust me?'

Hetty laughed. 'Of course I trust you. When a woman gets to my age, she can trust any man.' She clapped her hands twice. 'We'll have no more talk of broken glass. Ellen, you've been very quiet this afternoon, hardly a word, dear. You can introduce the next topic of conversation.'

Ellen looked away from their eyes. She could think of nothing new, nothing at all. She let the boy take the empty glass from her fingers. 'I don't know,' she said. 'Unless you want to talk about the English countryside.'

'Not of general interest, dear,' said Hetty.

'Gareth's been to England,' said Olive.

'Have you?' Hetty turned quickly. 'Have you really?'

'Briefly,' he said. 'For three weeks last year. We were in London most of the time but I saw a bit of the country. We had a few days travelling round the Lake District, and then for a couple of days we stayed with friends at Great Missenden in Buckinghamshire.' He poured from the decanter into their glasses. 'You'll know it a lot better than I do.'

'Oh yes, I adore the Cotswolds,' said Muriel. 'Did you get down to Aldershot?'

But he was looking at Ellen.

'No,' she said. 'I've never been to England.'

'Haven't you?' He seemed surprised and that pleased her.

'Mother and Daddy were both English, of course,' she said. 'But Hetty and I have never been outside of New Zealand.'

'We were considering a sea voyage a few years ago,' said Hetty. 'People advised us against it. They warned us we'd find the old country changed so much, we'd be disappointed.'

'Terribly,' said Muriel.

'Did you find it changed, Mr Malleson?' said Hetty.

'I don't know,' he said. 'I couldn't make a comparison. Everyone kept telling me the cities had altered beyond recognition but no one told me what they meant by it. Whether you'd be disappointed or not would depend on your expectation, I suppose.'

'But the countryside,' said Ellen, 'is it as green as they say it is?'

'Not when I was there,' he said. 'They were having a drought and the paddocks were burned to a crisp, more like the colour of Spain or Greece.'

Oh no, thought Ellen. Not paddocks. Fields. Fields and meadows, woods and copses, spinneys and hedgerows and thickets.

'These days,' said Muriel, 'you can go from the Bayswater Road to Regent Street and not see a Londoner.'

'Yes,' said the boy, passing their refilled glasses. 'I reckon you could. It's just about possible.'

'You haven't poured one for yourself,' said Hetty.

'No,' he said. 'I'd like to, but if you don't mind, it's time I excused myself.'

'So soon?' said Hetty.

'I'm sorry,' he said. 'I could happily stay here all afternoon.'

'He's taking the car into town,' said Olive.

'Oh yes,' said Hetty remembering. 'You have an appointment.'

He had stepped backwards. 'Thank you for the wine. It was great, really fantastic. And thank you for being so nice about the you-know-what. No, stay there. Please don't bother to get up.'

'Don't be any later than five on the dot,' said Olive.

He had moved beyond the trees but even in full sunlight he looked cool, as though he were made of shade itself. His right hand was palm out towards them, instructing them to remain seated, but when he reached the path he moved it in a sweeping circle and called, 'Ciao. See you later.'

After he'd gone they sat quietly for a while, sipping wine and listening to the sounds of bees in the garden. The air was hot and still and beyond the shadow of their tree the lawn shimmered at an uncertain level as though it were in the process of being dissolved.

On the table one of the red roses made a small noise like a sigh and dropped its petals all at once on to the white cloth.

'You must be very proud of him, dear,' Hetty said to Olive.

'I am,' said Olive. 'But I mean to say, I would be, wouldn't I? There's always something special about the first grandchild.'

'He's charming,' said Muriel.

'He didn't want to come in,' said Olive. 'I had to force him and after all that, I thought we'd never get rid of him. He looked — ha ha. Rid of him. Ridd. Oh, he lapped that up a treat, did you see? See him blush?'

Ellen put her glass back on the table. She felt exhausted, unreasonably tired, and yet at the same time wide awake as though she had narrowly missed some frightful danger. She rested her head back on the cushion and listened to the birds and insects. Somewhere in the garden a grey warbler had started up. It trilled on the upper register like a tipsy flautist, a beautiful extravagant sound.

'Are you ready?' said Muriel.

'Yes, please,' said Olive.

Muriel read in clear and careful tones, 'You may suppose that my heart beat high, when the King and Queen appeared, and entered, followed by the Duke of Norfolk, bearing the sword of state, and by several other noblemen and people of repute . . . '

Ellen shut her eyes.

It could almost have been a nightingale.

# DISTANCES

After the row they were kind to each other. He made two cups of coffee and asked if he should butter some water crackers. She gave the question more consideration than was necessary, then said, yes please, that would be very nice. They took a tray through to the sitting room and sat on either side of the coffee table, in separate patches of sunlight.

In earlier years, they'd had a physical alchemy to mend quarrels. In bed they had wrestled with their anger until it had fallen away, leaving them miraculously renewed. That no longer happened. It was not that they were too old, but, being old enough, they had become more skilled in warfare, and they inflicted on each other, wounds too severe for the rough encounter of bodies.

She sipped her coffee and ate a biscuit which tasted of dust. The sun poured the shape of the windows over the carpet and across her feet. A branch of the magnolia tree scraped a corner of the glass. Its dark green leaves, fired with light, were reduced to abstract movement on the far wall.

She couldn't taste the coffee either.

These days there was no shouting, no tears. They had long since made maps of the vulnerable areas so that now they knew how to wound with the slightest touch. They used silence and small politeness, gestures which to another might seem harmless. They hid poisoned darts in something they called duty.

Why do we do it? she thought, staring at the window. Why does it seem necessary?

He said, 'I must get the percolator fixed. I hate instant coffee.'

'Yes.' She looked in her cup, saw her reflection and thought of it as being freeze-dried. 'We must.'

'Do we need a new percolator?'

'No. It's just the element.'

'I'll take it in this week. Remind me, will you?'

'Don't worry. I'll attend to it.'

'It's out of your way.'

'Not really. I'll be using the car on Wednesday morning. I'll do it then.'

'As long as it's no trouble,' he said.

She realised that he, too, was avoiding a meeting of eyes. He finished his coffee and lit a cigarette, but instead of leaning back as was usual, he sat forward, hunched over his knees, turning the cigarette in the ashtray to wipe off ash barely formed. He said, 'Have you got much to do on Wednesday?'

'Where? Town? Not a great deal. The percolator element, new hooks for the curtains — Is there something you want?'

'If you've got the time, you might like to get the car serviced. It'll need a grease and oil change before we go to Rose's.'

She glanced at him, but his face offered nothing. 'Do you want to go?' she said, demanding truth.

'It's not a matter of wanting.' He sounded equally severe. 'She's expecting us, and that's that, we're committed. I suppose it's a possibility, once we're there, I might enjoy myself.'

'You won't. The children will drive you mad.'

'I'll shut myself in their TV room. I'll watch the football.'

'What about chess?'

'It's not important.' He raised his hand to stall her interruption. 'I'm not contradicting myself. I mean it's unimportant compared with Ricky's birthday party. He's expecting me. Kids remember things like that. I can play chess any Saturday I want.'

'Not in the tournament. Look, there'll be other birthdays and parties —'

'You said we were coming. Right? Right. So we'll go. Don't worry, relax, I'll be nice to my grandchildren, only I warn you, if those kids start screeching and throwing food round the place, I'm locking myself in with the TV.'

'What will happen about the tournament?' she insisted.

He waved the question away, but she knew that he was hurt and that the wound would lie between them for a long time.

She said, 'I can easily phone Rose.'

He put out the cigarette and stood up. 'Make sure, when you get the car serviced, you tell them to check the tyres.' He smiled gently. 'I'm going out to mow the lawns.'

She wanted to keep him there, talking, but there seemed little else to say. She took the cups back to the kitchen and washed them, and a short time later she heard the lawn mower on the front lawn.

The afternoon fell back to its own patterns. She unfolded the ironing table, plugged in the iron and went out to the line to bring in the washing. Skins, she thought as she untangled shirts and dropped them in the basket, our clothes feel and smell like skins. She set the basket down by the ironing table. She imagined herself as a flayed animal. They were both flayed animals. Here were their pelts, cured, dried, ready to be cut into shape for strangers. Then she blinked, for the image was excessive, so full of self-pity, it alarmed her. She turned the iron on to steam. She could phone Rose and explain.

Rose, we can't come. You know your father. We've had an awful row about it, and as far as I'm concerned, it's just not worth —

Rose, we can't make it next Saturday. I know, I said, I'm sorry, I forgot all about your father's chess tournament —

But as she stood there, ironing his shirt, she knew that if he didn't go to Rose's he wouldn't go anywhere. They'd sit in front of the television box until they could escape to sleep.

Rose, your father has given up his chess tournament to come through Saturday. If he's a bit, you know, please try and understand —

Rose, about Saturday, can you keep Ricky and Megan out of Dad's hair? I know they get excited but why do they, I mean, why do you let them carry on like that? Well, I think he's right. I'm not just sticking up for him. Won't you accept that he might know just a little bit about bringing up kids?

She put the shirt on a hanger, took another from the basket.

For a while he'd done his own ironing. When she'd started full-time work at the library, he'd taken over a number of the household chores, preparing the vegetables for dinner, cleaning the outside of the windows when he'd finished washing the car. He'd offered to do his shirts, and she, certain that his efforts would produce wrinkles and scorchmarks, agreed. But he was deft with an iron, something she had not known in twenty-eight years of marriage, and as he smoothed creases from collars, she felt betrayal. It was as though she had discovered the presence of a mistress.

She tipped the iron forward. It gurgled and erupted boiling water over the cloth, before settling to a steady hush of steam. She ran it over the tail of the shirt.

It was a truth, she thought, that marriage, like everything else, had a natural lifespan. If it got old and died before the partners involved, that was too bad, there was nothing one could do about it. Theirs had been a good marriage, at times very good, and she was grateful. Not every couple had been as happy as they.

She listened to the sound of the motor mower. It was no use getting morbid and fretting for what was past. Time went on. One had to be sensible about these things, or where would the world be, for heaven's sake?

She stood the iron up at the end of the board and gazed at it for a few seconds, then she dropped the shirt back in the basket and went to the front of the house.

He was walking determinedly up and down the lawn, behind the machine, his sleeves rolled up, his face set in concentration. Wet grass and smoke sprayed over his boots. The noise tore at the air.

She ran down the path, followed him along a shaved strip, and tapped on his shoulder. When he turned his head, she shouted in his ear.

He stopped and the engine raced. 'What?' he bellowed.

She felt embarrassed. 'I love you,' she shouted again.

He was still. A suddenness of something moved across his face. His eyes opened wide to take in the sun, and became lighter in colour. Then he smiled, and they were both wrapped up in laughter.

Left to itself, the mower carried on across the lawn, and stalled in the flower garden.

# HEART ATTACK

There was no room in the house for his grief. It was a pain too big to be contained within walls and yet there was nowhere else to go. He went from one doorway to another and back again, while June followed him, asking questions.

'Why didn't they send a cablegram? They're not that poor, surely. Nick? Couldn't someone have phoned?'

He stopped in the middle of the kitchen and shook his head. Not Papa. It was too soon. You hear that, Papa? There is too much between us that hasn't been done.

He swung his arms at his sides.

It is not possible for you, Papa, to be dead.

'When was it mailed?' said June. 'The postmark, Nick. Have a look at the date. Darling, please let me see the letter.'

She opened his fingers and took the ball of blue paper from him. She flattened the page on the table, smoothing the creases between her hands, then leaned over it, unable to read a word. Her hair fell forward hiding her face, and her backbone showed in the gap between her sweater and her jeans. Standing beside her, he remembered the first time he had taken her home to meet Papa. Nikis, my boy, she is beautiful, ah, such a beautiful peach, you lucky dog.

June lifted her hair away from her face. 'What does it say?'

'They buried him the day after — on the sixteenth.'

'No point in going over there now,' she said. 'Why didn't they let you know in time?'

'I couldn't have gone.'

'Your father's funeral? Oh Nick, we could have managed the fare somehow.'

'I told you — it was the day after.'

'It could have been postponed. They could have waited for you. We'd have booked you on the first flight to Athens.' She shook the letter in his face. 'I don't understand why they didn't let his son know.'

'It doesn't matter,' he said.

'Of course it matters! They're only distant cousins. They can't do this to you.'

'Look, will you stop going on about it?'

'Nick, don't you care?'

He took the letter from her, folded it and put it in his shirt pocket, next to the pain that crowded his ribs. Breathing hurt him. Words hurt. He started walking again. 'I don't remember those people. They don't remember me.' He slapped his hands together. 'When he was alive, that's when I should have gone. Every letter — when are you coming, when am I going to see my grandson?'

'Yes. Well. We didn't know he was going to have a heart attack, did we?'

She turned away, and he knew from the stubborn set of her shoulders, that she, too, was remembering the time Papa had come to stay. They hadn't know he intended to make his home with them. A holiday, they thought, Papa standing alone at the station with his old cardboard suitcase and his too-long raincoat, his grey hair set in brilliantine ridges.

Papa's small weakness, that. Perfumed hair cream. Lavender, rose, carnation, essence of violets. His pillow cases always looked like old fish and chip papers.

The smell of Papa's hair oil drifted along the platform, greeting him before he saw the outstretched hands.

'Nikis, Nikis, your father is a stubborn old fool. I was wrong to try and hold you and June. I know that now, huh? You are young. You have to move where your future is, your work, have your own house. For June, huh? She don't want the old house your Mama died in. So, it is time for me to give in, Nikis. You are the young bull, I am the old bull, and I give in to you. I sell the old place, come to live here with my family.'

'To live, Papa? Here? What about your friends?'

'So? I find new friends.'

'But Papa, you know there is no Greek community here. You'll be lonely.'

'Nikis, Nikis, the whole world is my friend.'


June was drying the dishes, her back to him. He put his hand on her shoulder. It had to be said.

'We did it to him. We drove him out.'

'Don't you start blaming me,' she snapped.

'I didn't say you. I said *we* did it to him. If we'd given him a home he'd have never have gone back there.'

'But you mean it was me, don't you?' She turned and he saw that she was close to tears.

'No, no. It was both of us. You didn't understand, and I was wrong.'

'Nick,' she said in a tight voice. 'That's the last time you tell me I didn't understand. I wasn't going to say anything. I made a promise. Don't come between father and son, I told myself. Because that's just it, Nick, I did understand. Before we got engaged everyone told me the same thing. Marry a Greek, they said, and you marry his whole family. You get them all, brothers, sister, uncles, aunts. But that didn't worry me. There was only your father, and I was quite prepared for us to live with him. I knew that was what you wanted.' She turned the dishes. 'I didn't know then what he was really like. I couldn't stand it. The way he looked at me. And once — once he did it in front of you, and all you did was laugh!'

'What are you talking about?'

She was crying.

'June?'

'He pinched my bottom!' Tears were running down her face. 'He was a dirty old man! I hated him!'

He stared at her, then he held out his hands, cupped, as though she might put in them some other explanation. 'You mean — are you telling me — that's what it was about?' He shook his head. 'This was the reason I sent him away?'

'You didn't see the way he stared!'

'You were beautiful. He loved your beauty. You hated him for this? No, June. No!'

She was sobbing.

His pain grew huge and choked him so that he could not trust himself to words. He turned and rushed out of the house, slamming the back door behind him.

He stopped by the gate and waited, wondering if she would come out after him. She didn't. There was no sound from the house. He opened the gate and turned into the street, head down, thumbs hooked in his pockets, walking simply to free the ache in his chest and keep his thoughts moving.

There were a number of people about, mowing lawns, cleaning cars, the things he usually did on a Saturday morning. He was hardly aware of them, so full were his thoughts of his father.

For nearly two years, in fact ever since he left, Papa had been as distant as a faded photograph. Now, in death, he was so close and so big that he filled all earth and sky, his voice louder than the traffic. Nikis! Nikis!

There was a low stone wall outside the church. He sat, leaned forward against his knees, and stared at the cracked pavement. At the base of the wall, a few tufts of grass held a drift of confetti. He rubbed it with his heel. Rice was neater. The birds ate it. They, too, were God's creatures.

Papa believed in God. He talked about him often as though God were a personal friend, benevolent, a bit of a rogue.

That was something else June didn't like. 'Why does he talk like that?' she'd said.

He got up quickly and started walking again. He needed a cigarette, but he'd left his pack on the kitchen table and he had no money with him. He'd go to the service station. Dave knew him. Dave would give him credit.

He crossed the street and walked round the cars that waited at the pumps. Saturday mornings were always busy here. He went to the office and waited, leaning against the doorway. As he folded his arms, he felt the crackle of thin paper in his pocket.

I know, Papa, it is a joke. You are doing this to me. I have not written for months, so you think, aha, you will teach me a lesson. Eh, Papa? This minute you are in the taverna with your sly old cronies, laughing your head off at the comedy of the year.

'Hello Nick.' Dave came in with a handful of money. 'What can I do for you?'

'Have you got any —' He cleared his throat. 'I'm out of cigarettes, Dave. I've left my cash at home.'

'No problem. They're up there. Help yourself.'

'Thanks. I'll — I'll need matches too. Fix you up Monday.'

'No hurry.' Dave closed the till and was about to go out again. He stopped, put his head on one side and said, 'Anything wrong? Hey — you don't look too hot!'

'I'm all right.' He held on to the doorway.

'You sure?'

'I'm sure.'

Dave came close, put a hand on his shoulder, and peered at him. 'I thought you were going to conk out then.'

'Yeah. I'll be okay in a minute.'

103

'You're sick, aren't you? Thought so. Bet you a dollar to a doughnut you're going down with that flu bug.'

He shook his head and closed his eyes against the rush of tears, then he put his head on Dave's shoulder and the pain came to the surface in howling sobs.

Dave shoved him inside the doorway. 'Nick! What's the matter? Cripes, man, what's happened?'

'Papa,' he said, against Dave's shoulder. 'He's dead. Papa's dead.'

'Your father?' Dave was trying to make him stand up straight. 'That's tough. I'm sorry to hear — look, Nick —'

'I sent him away, Dave. I broke Papa's heart.'

'Nick, come on! You're not a kid. Stop it!' And Dave slapped him over the ear.

He stepped back and put his hand against his face. 'I'm sorry.'

'Wipe your nose,' Dave said.

He had no handkerchief. He used his sleeve. 'Sorry, Dave.'

'You can't go out like that,' said Dave. 'Sit down. Now light a fag while I find out where they put my bottle. You got yourself churned up, didn't you?'

He sat in the chair by the cluttered desk. 'I'm sorry,' he was saying. 'Sorry.' But the tears kept coming, even though he was no longer crying.

'It's here somewhere,' said Dave, kneeling in front of a cupboard. 'Half a bottle of five star brandy.'

'Thanks. I don't need a drink.' He lit a cigarette. 'I should get home. I left June —'

Dave went on searching. 'I know it's here. In this office. Your father, isn't he the old fellow who went back to Greece?'

'Yes.'

'How did it happen? Heart?'

'Yes. It was very sudden.'

'That's a comfort, anyway. A long life and then out like a light before you know what hits you. That's the story. My old man died of cancer, and you wouldn't wish that on anyone.'

'I'm fine now,' he said. 'I'd better go.'

'Found it! I knew it was here.' Dave uncorked a bottle with his teeth and picked up a coffee mug. 'This'll do the trick,' he said, filling it almost to the brim. He passed it across. 'Get that inside you. Good for the shakes.'

He sipped to oblige him.

'Got to go out now and give the boys a hand. Just sit here and take your time, okay?'

'Thank you, Dave.'

Then he was out to the long line of cars and the pumps.

Oh Papa. Papa, don't leave me.

He watched the cigarette burn down. His eyes were hot and swollen and his nose was running. He didn't want brandy. He put the cup down and covered his face with his hands.

Papa, I remember at the wedding you were such a little man, your head with its curls and perfume, no higher than my shoulder. I could have picked you up in one hand. Then you started to grow and I began to shrink, smaller, smaller. Now you are as big as the world and I am just a little kid, a baby. No, Papa, I am less. I am nothing. My house is nothing. My new car is nothing. My wife, my son, my job.

The trouble was, Papa, you lived on one side and she lived on the other. Neither of you could understand what it was like for me in the middle. The man who stands in the middle has no country. He is nothing.

He put out the cigarette and stood up, leaving the cup of brandy on the desk. He went out the back way, through the workshop, into the yard, down the alley to the road.

Then he was in the door and standing in the kitchen with June still beside the bench, back at the beginning of it all. But this time she didn't hammer him with questions. She looked at him for a moment, then came and put her arms round his waist, her head on his chest.

One winter, he couldn't remember which one, he and Papa visited Mama's grave nearly every Sunday to pray, and then they

105

would both blow their noses on Papa's best white handkerchief.

By her grave, he had asked, 'Is Mama an angel now, Papa?'

'Nikis, your mother was born an angel. When you are growed up you will understand, all women are angels. It's the way God makes them — with big loving hearts. Now a man, sometimes he has nothing to give to a woman. But the woman, she can always give to the man. Remember that.'

'Yes, Papa, I'll remember.'

June's head was beneath his chin, her hair flowing down over his shirt like scented silk. He touched the crown of her head with his lips.

She said, 'You are shivering.'

'Yes.'

'Are you cold?'

He nodded.

'I'll make you a cup of coffee,' she said.

'Don't leave me!' He tried to hold her.

'Nick, let go! You're hurting me!' She pulled away.

His arms fell at his sides, and he began to cry again. He sniffed and wiped his face against his arm. He was tired of saying he was sorry, but there was nothing else to say.

# GOING TO THE
# MOUNTAIN

'This winter I'll take you to the mountain,' his father said. While the boy knelt on the chair at the window, watching the grey lines of rain angle in against the hut. Which was very strange, because although the boy's eyes had been fastened open by the monotony of the rain, he'd been thinking about the same thing. It lay there behind the wetness, behind the water-filled bootprints at the back door, the axe, the firewood heap, the dripping fences, behind the paddocks full of grey sheep, a vision of a marvellous mountain with snow as dry as sugar.

He thought of it often, this mountain. It seemed to be always somewhere within him, a peak of perfect whiteness in a clear blue sky, and now his father, unknowing, had struck the hollow of its hiding place with a blow so precise that it opened right out, spilling whiteness into the room. With a rush it came, all of it at once, snowflakes as big as dinner plates, scissors-cut, icicles chiming in the cupboards and under the beds, drift upon drift whirling inside and out until the entire hut was sliding away in an avalanche with him kneeling at the centre, frozen rigid to the back of the chair.

'What do you say?' his father said. 'A train trip to Ruapehu?
See some snow?'

The boy had no breath for answer. The feeling of cold was
intense on his back and there was a melting in his eyes which
blurred his sight. His father shimmered in the orange light of the
fire, and the boy wanted to get past the snowdrifts to reach him.
There was no fear of his father at that moment. He wanted to
hook his arms round his father's neck and squeeze, shouting,
'When? When?' But the cold had locked his hands on the back of
the chair and, although he fought it as hard as he could, he knew
from the sliding away that the thing was happening again.

When he woke up, he was lying on a sack in front of the fire.
The sound of rain was everywhere and his father's feet were close
by, flat on the floor and unmoving. He stared at the socks,
wrinkled khaki stuck with hay seeds, stared and quietly wept.
He didn't hurt anywhere but the thing always left him with a
feeling of sadness and so tired that he could have been walking
across the paddocks for miles in a gale force wind. He lay with his
thumb in his mouth, his forefinger round his nose, and cried until
his father nudged him with his foot.

'You wet yourself,' said his father. 'You'd better get changed.'

He sat up slowly, touching the dampness at his middle, then
he crawled on his hands and knees to his bed and the box beside
it which held his clothes. His father didn't look at him while he
changed his pants. He put on some old grey shorts that Ro had
given him last year, no buttons on them, her brother's cast-offs,
she'd said. Then he went back to sit at the fire. His father gazed at
the flames and worked his jaw from side to side as though he
were eating his own teeth. The boy watched him for a while.
'When are we going to the mountain?'

The man stopped the jaw movement but didn't look at him.
'What'd you say?'

'I said, when are we going to the mountain to see real snow?'

'Oh. Soon. Pretty soon.'

'Tomorrow?' said the boy. 'Next week?'

'I dunno,' said the man. 'When the weather clears up. When I can manage a few days off. You change those britches?'

'Yes.' But the boy couldn't let it go at that. He stood up, clutching the front of his shorts where the buttons were missing, and went to the wall calendar. 'Next week's sure to be fine. Not much work now until lambing starts. Feeding out — Mr Grant could do that. Dad, what about next weekend?'

'Maybe,' said his father. He looked at the boy, then turned away again to the fire. 'Hang your britches out in the rain,' he said. 'Go on. Don't leave them on the floor to stink the place out.'

They didn't go to the mountain that weekend or at any other time. The boy was too young to realise that the promise had been a gift in itself, quite detached from any intention of fulfilment. Like the talk of a pony or a new wireless set, the offer had been prompted by guilt, for although the man was known to be harsh, he wasn't a vindictive person, and when he caught himself loathing his son, he would extend some generous words in atonement.

But the boy didn't know this. Each fine winter's day brought its own hope, and when the next weekend passed without mention of the trip, he fastened on the weekend after and all the others following it on the wall calendar.

He was eager to tell Ro. He watched for her and ran to meet her, grabbing her hand and swinging on her arm: 'Dad's taking me to the mountain!'

'Hey you, take it easy,' she said. 'Don't go getting all het up.'

'We're going to the mountain. Dad and me. I'm going to make a snowman.'

'When's this?' said Ro, stopping and holding both his hands to make him face her. She was wearing a red skirt that made her look fat and she had red ribbons in her black hair. She never wore shoes. Summer or winter she came across the grass barefooted to clean their hut, do their once-a-week wash, all from the goodness of her heart. Ro had a heart as big as a barn, his father said. She was also very pretty.

'How long you going for?' she wanted to know.

'Couple of days, I think. Dad says as soon as he can get time off.'

'Oh yeah. Well, you stop jumping up and down like a rabbit or you know what. Your Dad, he's working right now?'

'No, he's inside.'

Ro laughed and put her arm around his shoulders, drawing him close until his head was against her red skirt. 'I'll go and make us a cuppa.'

She didn't greet the man, nor he her. She put the kettle on the fire, then got the boy to stack dishes while she pumped water into the tin basin.

The man had a newspaper on the table and was waterproofing his boots on it, greasing them with a rag dipped in mutton fat. He said to her, 'That one had another fit last Wednesday.'

Ro went on pumping. 'You belted him.'

'Didn't lay a finger on him. Didn't so much as raise my voice. There was nothing started it — that right?' he looked at the boy. 'He just set off by himself.'

The boy stacked the dishes carefully, knowing that if he was quiet, they would forget about him. Ro went to the table and leaned across it. 'It's not good for him here. He should be at school.'

'He does his lessons.'

'He needs more than lessons. He needs other kids, a bit of decent care.'

'Can't afford it,' said the man.

'Course you can. You're a miserable so-and-so. You treat him like one of those dogs. You don't talk to him unless you get mad at him or want him to fetch something. You're real rotten.'

The boy stood still, holding a plate to his chest.

His father pointed to him. 'Just as well he isn't my dog. By jingo, if a dog did that to me, I'd put a bullet through his head.'

He winked at the boy and laughed, pleased with his own joke.

The boy laughed took, looked at the floor and giggled, the plate grasped in both hands.

Ro couldn't see the funny side. She grabbed the boy and held his face against her stomach, saying, 'Don't you listen to that useless no good. He's just talking a lot of big fat stink. Just pretending, eh. Just rubbish.'

His father went on laughing, a deep and rare sound. He stood up, his hands on the table, and said, 'Let him go, will you? Time he went for a walk.'

The boy looked up at Ro for support, but none was coming. She ruffled his hair, took the plate away and gave him an empty billy tin. 'Go down to the creek and get some watercress for tea.'

'I thought you were making us a cuppa.'

'Later on,' she said. 'You know, for when you get back.'

He glanced at his father, then dragged at Ro's arm until she bent her head to him. Holding her hair away from his mouth, he whispered, 'Tell him. Ask him. About taking me to the mountain.'

She straightened up. 'All right. But don't you be in any hurry to get back.'

'Okay.'

He closed the door behind him and waited on the steps until he heard the scraping of the bolt inside, then he went out through the gate, past the dogs that barked and leapt on their chains, past the hen-house and towards the creek, and it seemed to him that every step he made left a print in fresh white snow.

Perhaps Ro believed there would be a trip to the mountain, or perhaps she simply augmented the promise to please him. He never knew. But for the rest of that winter she knitted him a jacket from the fleece of a black sheep. To wear in the snow, she said.

The knitting made the journey a certainty for him. He sat at her feet while she pulled tufts from the fleece and rolled them into yarn against her thigh. Then she hooked the thread into the garment with sharpened bits of fencing wire.

His father would come in from the lambing round, cold, wet, in a bad mood. 'You still doing that? What about a feed?'

Ro would say calmly, 'Don't you come at me with that bossy stuff. I'm not your fancy woman.'

Only Ro could talk to the man like that without making him angry. She would go on knitting and the man would slump in his chair and close up his face.

The boy used to say, 'It's getting near the end of winter.'

And Ro would answer, 'Got to wait till your jacket's finished, eh.'

That was how he remembered it in later years, and although as an adult he saw half the mountains of the world, he was always deeply disappointed. Not even the majestic peaks of the Himalayas could meet the expectation he had carried with him from his childhood. It seemed to him that every part of those years on the farm with his father, the hills, the dogs, the shepherd's hut, the ribbons in Ro's hair, everything whispered messages of snow, everything pointed to a mountain too rare for the world.

At a time in his life when he could no longer relive or even remember the excitement of that exquisite anticipation, the dreams of the mountain began. The first came soon after his wife died. He was in a glass bubble, a cable-car of the type he'd seen in Switzerland, slung on a cable track, doors at either side, full of people dressed for skiing. To begin with he didn't know why he was there, then, as the cable-car swung through the clouds, he felt a joy so keen that it stuck in his chest like a knife blade. He was going. After the years, he was finally going. And oh, the indescribable pleasure of recognition as the cable-car broke cloud and he saw in front of him a wall of white ice as smooth as marble. He pressed his hands against the glass and absorbed the chill of it until he was tinkling and sparkling with frost.

'It's as I've always known it!' he cried, his breath exploding in fine crystals. 'How could there have been any doubt? Ro! Ro, do you see it?'

Ro stood amongst the people, smiling politely as though embarrassed by his lack of control.

'We're almost there!' he shouted at her.

Then he realised that the car was not slowing down. Indeed, its speed had increased and now it was travelling so fast that the ice face was a blur.

'No!' He beat on the glass doors, tried to kick them apart, while the other passengers watched, and Ro still smiled, her head on one side.

'Stop! I want to get out!'

It was too late. The temperature increased as they plunged into cloud again and in a moment there was nothing outside but a thick oppressive greyness.

Still, he did retain something of the journey. For days afterwards there was something like a wound in his chest where he'd suffered near-perfect ecstasy.

After that his dreams took him near the mountain a number of times, but in a lesser way, on foot and guided only by the expectation, that silence in him which was the hush of snow, or else the smell of snow in the air. It could happen on any kind of road and in the height of summer, a walk interrupted by something which quivered in him like the needle of a Geiger counter, and, sniffing the air, he would turn off through some orchard or lawn, forest or ploughed field, following the instinct he'd learned to trust. They were never easy, these journeys in sleep, especially that last slope where his feet became cramped and heavy and each step was a struggle through thick dark scrub or knotted grasses. But when he got beyond that and saw the vast white expanse in front of him, the discomfort would leave him and he'd be filled with the sweetest yearning.

That feeling of longing, like his sense of snow, did not exist for him outside of these dreams; but the remembering of them in waking hours did build a bridge directly to his childhood. It was a marvel to him that memories of those harsh years with his father, could give him more satisfaction than the comparative comfort of adult life. Childhood was the time of snow.

Ill health forced him into retirement at fifty-eight. He sold the house and bought a small cottage a few streets distant from his eldest daughter who liked to manage him. She was a good soul like her mother, but noisy and efficient. She, her husband and their three children had all been blessed with loud voices. Sometimes, when he saw them coming, he locked the door.

One night, a week after his sixty-third birthday, he went to the mountain in an aeroplane. It was a DC10 and he was sitting with a crowd of people on a flight that could have been going anywhere, he didn't know; but when the air in the cabin became suddenly, inexplicably cold, he felt a small pain of hope. A few minutes later he was certain. The cabin lights dimmed and went out, the rest of the passengers disappeared. He was sitting alone with his face against the frozen glass, his heart beating out loud with the jubilant sound of new-year bells.

The wing-tip stirred the ink-blue universe, scattering stars so that they spun away from the leading edge in showers of silver dust. Inside, everything glittered with frost. The tops of the seats were ridged with white and luminous in the dark. In the rack above his head, his felt hat glistened like a wedding cake.

The bells tolled about his ears with greater vigour, reaching a fullness as the mountain came into view. It was not beneath him as he'd expected but bigger, higher than he'd seen it before. It reached above the aircraft, a tower of ice so close he marvelled that the wing did not touch it. How beautiful it was, glowing in its own white light, and how immense its coldness. While the wing-tip skimmed that sheer white wall, he felt powerful with rapture, and when at last the mountain receded into the night, he knew better than to weep with disappointment.

The next morning he felt the need to talk to his daughter, to have a conversation that went beyond housekeeping and pills, to find out, if the truth be known, just who his daughter was. He phoned and invited her over but she was busy. She was always busy. He said he needed to talk to her. She said, go ahead.

Messages, he said. He needed some messages done. She told him, you should have said that in the first place, and later that day she sent her eldest son over with a jar of marmalade.

The boy was nine years old and had a bullying stare. He walked right in and helped himself to an apple from the sideboard.

'What are you doing here? I asked your mother to come.'

'She can't,' said the boy. 'She's got her work to do.'

'I don't want you. Go back home.'

The boy stood his ground. 'She said I had to get you your messages.'

'I don't want anything. Please go back and tell my daughter I have something to say to her.'

The boy bit the apple with a wrenching sound. 'She won't come.'

'All right, tell her this. Tell her I've had a bad turn.'

'But you haven't. Have you?'

He thought for a moment. 'No.'

'You're wanting me to tell lies,' said the boy.

'Is that so?' He tried to match the boy's insolence. 'And what will you be when you've finished chopping down cherry trees? Tinker, tailor, beggarman, thief?'

The boy was either too clever or too stupid for sarcasm. He shrugged. 'Don't know yet. probably a lawyer like Dad. What do you want me to get at the shops?'

'Nothing. I told you — not a thing. Wait a minute, boy.' He stepped in front of him and put his hand on his shoulder, felt softness, fat over bone. 'Did you know that my father — your great-grandfather — was a shepherd? I grew up in a one-roomed shepherd's hut, no hot water, no stove. Did all the cooking on the open fire —'

The boy's face went blank.

'I was ten before I went to school. Know that? Such education as I had out there, came from the correspondence school in Wellington.'

'You told me,' said the boy, wriggling to free himself. 'Thousands of times.'

'Stand still when I talk to you! And look at me! That's better. Tell me this — have you ever been to the mountain?'

'Sure.'

'When?'

The boy frowned. 'You know.'

'Damn it all, boy, do you think I'm asking for the fun of it?'

'You do so know. Aw, Grandad, you came up with us once. Skiing with Mum and Dad up Ruapehu.'

'Not that! I don't mean one of your heaps of trampled confection —' He stopped, forgetting what he was going to say. It didn't matter. The boy couldn't possibly understand. He released him and waved him towards the door. 'There's nothing I need. Thanks for calling in.'

The boy shrugged. 'Mum says don't let the marmalade get mouldy.'

'I won't. Tell your mother she's very kind and I'm grateful.'

He went a little way down the path and watched his grandson saunter down the street, eating his apple. The child was solidly built, large backside and thick straight legs, blond hair like his father.

He turned and went back to the house.

By the front porch he stopped, hand on the railing, to look at a geranium bush which had grown large with bright red flowers. Grasping the railing firmly, he leaned over until his face was against the flowers, and he was surprised to discover that already, they smelled of snow.

# ALL ABOUT LOVE

I find it difficult to write in this room; it is so small and dark and the heavy bladed fan on the ceiling groans and shudders, coughs against the edges of my writing paper and disturbs my hair with its struggling breath. Yet, if I turn it off I will not be able to write at all. Who was it who told me that Delhi would be cool this time of year?

I can scarcely see the ink on the page. What light dribbles in through the slats of the shutters, is soaked up by the green painted walls. I call the colour Indian green because it is seen everywhere in this country, a rich green with a depth of jade to it — except that in this room it is peeling away from the plaster and, at floor level, has been spattered by pan chewers. Betel juice mixed with sputum looks like blood. On my first day here I thought there had been a knife fight on the stairs.

For the life of me, I cannot concentrate. I suppose I could open the shutters but then the afternoon light would rush in, blazing white, to bleach out the entire work before it is written. Darkness is better, I think, for a short story set back in New Zealand on a cool winter's day. Where would two people meet on such a day? A coffee shop, yes, white wrought-iron tables with

JOY COWLEY

gingham cloths and blue and white china, ferns hanging in baskets by a window washed with rain. I can see it from the outside, the glow of the interior, the rain sweeping against the leadlight glass in great gusts which blur and melt the faces at a near table.

The story is all about love, and quite simple. These two people met many years ago, discovered a compelling attraction, did not act on it and then accidentally or mistakenly married other partners. Brought together again a few years later, they became lovers and stole the fire of the gods. Oh, but they were made of flame, those two. They would burn up their afternoons and each other in their passion and everything was fuel for their love. They were sure that they could never live without each other and at one stage considered throwing two marriages into that all-consuming fire. Then something happened, I'm not sure what, and they were separated for a long time, twenty, twenty-two years. Perhaps they lived in different countries. Anyway, they did not see each other until fate brought them together for the third time. Now she is divorced; his wife has died. Here they are, middle-aged, meeting again in this little coffee shop, wrapped in rain.

Although the story is straightforward, I would like it to have many layers so that it can be peeled with each reading to give some new truth about love. What each truth will be, can vary with the reader, but there'll always be recognition. That's the thing with truth. It is instantly familiar. And when all the skins of the story have been peeled like the layers of an onion, then there will appear the last truth, that little green shoot which is the truth of our being, and in that there will be the ultimate statement about loving.

After four false starts, I've got them at the table, shy as strangers. She has a long aquiline face, straight greying hair and a red beret spotted with rain. She sits forward, with her shoulders drawn up to her ears, picking at the threads of the tablecloth with pointed red-lacquered nails. She has beautiful eyes, light grey, dark shadowed, which she hides from him in her shyness. He has thick curly hair, also grey, and has grown to flesh which suits him. He fills all the spaces between them with talk about the weather and when she makes comment, he eagerly agrees and wipes his lips with his forefinger as though trying to find a way to get his mouth into second gear. That is the problem. I have them in this potentially powerful situation but I can't draw them together in a real conversation. They sit waiting for their coffee, for each other, for me, while all the time the rain hurls itself against the window (sounding not unlike the fan in this room) and she is newly embarrassed to remember that on such a wet afternoon, more than twenty years ago, she bathed his body in champagne. She averts her eyes. The fire of her memories does not belong to this man. He, discomforted by her coolness, is clumsy in his movements. He drops the black umbrella he has propped against his chair and in leaning down to retrieve it, he pulls the tablecloth and upsets a small vase. A waitress picks up scattered carnations and mops away the water, saying that she will put a clean cloth on the table, but they insist, talking over each other, that it doesn't matter. They seem glad to have the waitress with them and ask her questions about her work. Where does she live? Is the place busy in summer? When she goes, they return to their awkward remarks about the weather. I don't know how to release them.

I drop pen and exercise book and wipe my hands. It is not possible to enter the fullness of the story in this dark room with solid chunks of stale air beating at my face. Everything in here irritates me, the furtive gait of the cockroaches, the beads of sweat which crawl on my skin. Outside the door, voices pass in fragments of Hindi, faceless, unanswered, and suddenly I am overwhelmed by a feeling of imprisonment. I pull back the wooden shutters at the window. It is like opening the door of a noisy oven. The white light of the afternoon rushes in with the roar of traffic and immediately I am affected by the heat.

The street down there is thickly paved with movement: buses and trucks and taxis, rickshaws, pony traps, ox carts heaped high with bales of cotton, scooters, bicycles, sacred cows sniffing hopefully in the windows of cars, barrows, children, beggars. Over it all hangs a pall of yellow dust and above that hover the dark crows, their cries penetrating the traffic noise.

The buildings on either side of the road are either under construction or else falling down. As my friend Dr Varadan says, Delhi is a city of ruins, some of them old, some of them new. I think of it as a city of ceaseless activity, of large trees, and buildings which look as though they've been made of tea-stained sugar cubes.

The waitress has brought my characters their coffee, but that does not help the story. What I have written contains no inspiration, only deletions and patches of sweat.

It's useless trying to write up here.

I take pen and exercise book, lock the door behind me, and go down the three flights of stairs — see, fresh betel nut juice on the landing? — down to the desk where the two Sikh brothers who run this guest house, are drinking glasses of tea. They have the genuine smiles of children as they call out their greetings, 'Hello, hello, Madam. *Namaste.*'

They think I am mad which makes them very friendly, but they were not always so relaxed. Europeans do not usually come to a guest house in this part of town unless they have blackmarket goods or American dollars for sale, or they want to buy drugs. The Sikhs stopped pestering me when they learned I was a writer. This country understands writers.

By the door of the guest house, in the shade at the edge of the wide footpath, is a wooden bench where I sometimes sit to watch the traffic. People live out their lives on this pavement, eating, sleeping, working, coupling, giving birth and dying amongst the many little stalls which change character throughout the day. In the morning, when the sun hangs over the buildings like a huge red balloon, and the sleepers are still huddled together in rows, the tea vendors call, '*Chai, chai, chai!*' and there are bright charcoal burners cooking *puris* for early risers. The shoe-shine boys are busy. Men sell oats for horses. The pony men who have

slept the night in their traps, yawn, scratch their heads and clear
their noses, cough, spit, tune their voices for the day in laughter
as they polish their harness.

By mid-morning there are fruit stalls, stationery sellers, shirt
and sari merchants, people mending tyres or collecting bundles of
rags or burning incense at tiny shrines decked with marigolds.
Mothers wash children at the pumps at the edge of the pavement;
people squat in drains; homespun cotton is hung out in hanks to
dry. Towards evening, the place is given over to food stalls and the
sacred cows push through the crowds to search for vegetable
peelings.

The children know me. They come in twos and threes like
little pigeons, wanting to touch my clothes, my hair, look at my
pen, try on my sandals. As one lot grows tired of me, another lot
arrives. They are beautiful and it is not their fault that I lack
concentration. Even here, where the air is cooler and there is a
great pouring out of life energy all about me, even here I cannot
unlock the characters in the story. They remain fixed.

To compensate, I try describing them minutely, the way the
woman shakes her head slightly before answering a question, the
way the light from the man's white shirt is reflected upwards
against his skin, giving him a look of innocence. It seems to her
that this man sitting on the other side of the table shares none of
her memories, that in his mind there is only his dead wife and his
family. There is a pain inside her which she can't identify, but
later she will realise that it is grief for two people who ceased to
exist at that meeting.

But no, I don't want it to be that way. I want them to come
together again. It is important that there be a discovery not
simply of the people they are now, but of the fact that it was their
love which made them thus. I don't want to use the cliché
'searing passion' but the whole point of the story is that
their fire gave them transcendence. It was the intensity of
their lovemaking which caused some sort of metallurgical
transformation and made them into higher beings, creatures with

a knowledge of the infinite. They must be able to recognise that, and when they leave the coffee shop they will go to his apartment to create a new phoenix from the ashes.

There is a small commotion down the street. A horse has collapsed between the shafts, dead, I think. I can't see for the instant crowd which surrounds it. Everyone cries out and gesticulates as though witness to murder, while the traffic banks up on either side and voices are accompanied by a full orchestra of horns.

The time must be close to half past four because Dr Varadan is walking home from his surgery. He runs a clinic not far from here, another of those sugar cube buildings with upper storeys occupied by families, and buffalo grass drying on the roof.

They seem to be dragging the dead horse to the side of the road. I stand up to see better. Dr Varadan greets me with the palms of his hands pressed together, and I sit down again. He settles on the bench beside me and asks if I am writing letters to my family. I say, no, I am trying to write a short story. He asks, what sort of story?

'It's about — about people.'

'Most stories are about people.'

'No. Not most. I think a lot of stories are about events and the people come into them as scenery or furniture.' I close the exercise book when he tries to read what I've written. 'It's not going very well. In fact, it's not going at all.'

'What is wrong with it?' His interest contains a practical understanding. Since his wife died three years ago he has been writing poetry; but he says there is nothing unusual in that, everyone in India is a poet.

'The characters won't fit into the plot. They're real enough, but they're independent. They won't come together.'

His smile is gentle. He is a thin man with a finely crafted face and eyes which seem always on the verge of tears. He has supple bony hands which shape the air as he speaks. 'The best way to begin is with the heart.'

'Yes, but it's a matter of finding the heart. Sometimes it's well hidden.'

'These characters,' he says, 'there are two of them, a man and a woman. Yes?'

'Yes. Oh look, they've brought a cart to take away the dead horse.'

He doesn't look. 'They are in love with each other?'

'They were. Many years ago. It was a very important love affair. It ruled their lives. Then they were separated for a long time and when they met again, it seemed — I don't know — it just seems that they are intimidated by the past. Perhaps the changes are too great or different from the ones they expected. I don't even know what they expect. And yet, when the story first came to me, it was clear enough. Yes — but I shouldn't talk about it. It's all too easy to talk out a story and leave nothing for the writing.'

He nods. 'In life also it is a very big problem. Yes, for us Indians too, and we are a very emotional people. We don't hide away our feelings. But the older we get, the harder it is. The mind likes its stillness. It doesn't want the heart to jump into love and take those risks again. The heart cries out for the past. The mind remembers the inconvenience of it. The heart says, give me the ecstasy. The mind says, what about the pain? And because experience makes us a little cautious, we tend to listen more to the mind. Is that what is happening to your characters?'

'I don't know. It could be.'

'Of course, the way of the mind is the way of age, pointing to death. We know this also. That is why there is always a struggle going on. Listen, I will tell you a little poem.' He leans closer and his breath smells of spices. 'It is something like this — The mind is a pure white pearl, the body is a burning lamp. These two have nothing in common, and yet they constantly steal from each other.'

His face is so near mine that his features are blurred, but I am aware of his skin, smooth as brown stone, the pinkness inside his mouth, the warm breath scented with cardamom seeds. I turn away and ask, 'You've had another busy day?'

He laughs. 'Oh yes! Every day is busy. I am so very busy I should be the richest doctor in Delhi. The trouble is that my patients have no money and I get paid in rice and bananas.' He puts his hand over mine. 'If the story is not creating well, then maybe you will have time for tea with me in my surgery.'

I don't answer.

'I would be very happy if you would. You did say one day this week, and here it is not easy for us to talk with the noise. Will you come?'

'I'm sorry. Not today.'

'Please?'

I like his eyes. They warm me. I shake my head and withdraw my hand. 'No, thank you. It's very kind of you, but I must work on this.' And I hold the exercise book against me.

'Then we will have tea another day.' He stands and bows. 'I have written some poems for you. When you come to tea I will read them to you. Goodbye. I hope you finish your story.'

He walks away, tall, thin, slightly stooped, his brown shirt worn threadbare across the back.

The ox cart carrying the dead horse goes past. Two men walk behind, involved in some argument which is taken up by people on the footpath as they pass. The horse lying on the cart has its eyes open, and it quivers with the movement, as though it is still alive. I am aware that the air smells of animals and traffic fumes. Dust clouds the afternoon sun.

I don't know why I came down here. There is too much distraction, too much noise.

I would be better, after all, writing in my room.

# THE MACHINERY
## OF DREAMS

The year is 1954: I am seventeen and certain of my maturity. The place is the backyard of our family home at 32 Union Street, Foxton.

My father is at his sawbench cutting wood. The blade screams through logs, changing pitch against nails and pockets of sand; but Dad has been deaf since the age of twenty and hears none of it. When I tap him on the shoulder, he switches off the saw. I write on a scrap of paper, *Can I have a motorbike?*

'What'll you do for money?' he asks.

I scribble, *I'll save.*

One side of his face lifts in a laconic smile. 'Aye, the blazes ye will. Too many bluidy books.'

The truth of it makes me angry. I am in the first year of a pharmacy apprenticeship, earning £3.5s a week. £2 goes on board, a small amount on Pharmacy College fees, and the rest disappears in the local bookshop.

I underline the last two words on the paper, then add, *I'll work at nights and weekends.* I add in large letters, *please.*

Dad grins. 'We'll see how ye mend ye'r spendthrift ways.'

My mother is entertaining in the kitchen. As I go in, she shouts over the noise of the saw, 'What did he say?'

'I'm allowed to,' I yell back.

Her friend from the Ladies Guild says with an anxious laugh, 'Young ladies don't ride motorbikes.'

'I do,' I tell her.

'She's got her licence,' says my mother. 'We all reckon she should have been a boy. She can use a hammer and saw just as good as her father, lay concrete, do soldering — no different from a boy —'

I go into my bedroom, fall onto the bed and listen to her voice coming through the wall. I've heard the words so often my mouth can anticipate the shape of them.

'— it was never any good putting her in a decent dress. She'd rip it getting over the nearest barbed-wire fence or wrestling with the rough children at school. You could never keep her tidy. A real tomboy. If I dressed her in sugar sacks she wouldn't have cared.'

But she did care. She cared, she cared.

Throughout childhood I had a deep yearning for beautiful clothes, for ribbons and laces and dresses with ruffles. Why was it not possible to have this as well as bows and arrows?

These days the mirror shows a solid girl with a plain round face and turned up nose; but that is only the external view. Underneath she is slender, graceful and devastatingly beautiful. She has French perfume and fine lace underwear, an Edwardian dress of yellow silk with mutton-chop sleeves and tiny pearl buttons, a picture hat covered with veiling and gold silk roses, and she is riding through the town on a BSA 650 Gold Flash.

The main street of Foxton lies to the sun, broad as the back of a whale, normally so quiet that we get to know cars the way we recognise voices. Our ears prick at the piston slap of an A40, Mrs Meldrum coming in to get a dressing on her ulcer. We hear Dobby Baker's truck is on the way to the Post Office Hotel. But in January, that's when the alien traffic comes in and the town goes mad with people. The beach, three miles away, fills up with holiday-makers from Palmerston North and Wellington, and when they get bored with the sea, they come into the township to spend money. They're different sort of people from us, not lah-de-dah, just different, and sometimes we feel embarrassed for them. They go into the Pacific grill-room and ask for things like rare steak, or oysters cooked without batter, or black coffee. Or else the ladies want to know where the nearest rest room is, meaning lavatory, and we don't know how to tell them there's only the one in the children's playground where you wouldn't go without gumboots.

On Friday nights the beach people come in and rent the entire town. The street is solidly lined with Consuls and Zephyrs, Veloxes, Crestas, and a few of the posh ones, Daimler, Studebaker, Alvis Grey Lady, a new Austin Princess. Teenagers crowd the milk-bar and the jukebox spills out the voices of Teresa Brewer, Mario Lanza and Patti Page. Men stand in groups at the edge of the pavement, with the younger children. The women come into the pharmacy to buy bathing caps and other things.

Now, if a local woman wants an item of a very personal nature, she waits until the shop is empty, or else passes a note across the counter. The holiday woman is different. She says in a loud voice, 'And a packet of Tampax please.'

I blush for her. 'Regular or super?' I murmur.

'Super!' she exclaims.

I take the box from under the counter and am about to rewrap it, when she says, 'While I'm here, I'd better take a tube of Koromex cream.'

The shop is crowded. My face burns and words dry up. I open the you-know-what drawer in front of a dozen pairs of eyes and take out a pink box. I am not sure how this stuff is used but I do know why it's used. Everything in that drawer is associated with an activity which has no name except one too bad to repeat.

Years ago, when my sisters and I first found out about it, we called it pompom. I don't know why. Pompom was what people did to make babies, and it was our word. We could use it in public. Our parents didn't know what we meant or why we rolled about in laughter.

Childish words have a habit of sticking. In moments of embarrassment, the you-know-what becomes the pompom drawer.

Every Friday night Mr Fetridge comes in for his indigestion tablets. Mr Fetridge is an old and gentle widower with silver hair and a face like a seamed pumpkin, and although he shops in the same places every Friday night, he always dresses up for the outing in a suit with a bow-tie and a flower in his buttonhole. He has a black hat, and carries an umbrella.

'Good evening. Awfully close, isn't it? Do you think there's rain in the air, or does a storm merely brood in my imagination? I detect an excess of night-flying insects and that is, I believe, an indication of pending rain. The tummy tablets, if you please.'

As I wrap the tin, he puts an extra half-crown on the counter and asks for something else.

I don't understand.

He repeats it, then sensing my lack of comprehension, says, 'Perhaps you should fetch the chemist.'

I go into the dispensary and say to Mr Reddie, 'Mr Fetridge wants — he says — french something or other —'

Without a word, my boss hands me the prescription he is filling, and goes into the shop. I hear him open the pompom drawer. I hear more talk about the weather.

When he returns, Mr Reddie tells me matter-of-factly that french letters is another name for the male contraceptive Durex.

I don't answer, or even look at him, but later I have the chance to talk to Marjorie, the shop girl. She is three months younger than I, but she's been working for three years and she understands these things.

'He's old!' I tell her. 'He — he's not even married.'

Marjorie raises her thin shoulders, then lets them drop with a sigh. 'Why don't you grow up?' she says.

That night, I can't wait to tell my sister Joan what french letters are. I'm disappointed to discover that she has known for years. The children used to bring them to school, she said, and blow them up over the water tap. But I score a hit when I tell her who bought them.

'Old Mr Fetridge?' Her eyes widen and her tone becomes shrill. 'He's older than Dad. He must be fifty!' Then her voice goes into a squeak. 'He hasn't got a wife!'

I shrug with immense satisfaction. 'What difference does that make?'

At eight o'clock in the morning the flax mill stars up. The machines settle to a steady cry, wo-ow, wo-ow, wo-ow, as bunches of flax are fed through the strippers. The mouth of the stripper looks like the intake of a kitchen mincer and if a man gets his finger caught, it's off at the joint, quick as a wink. Woolpack & Textiles pay generous compensation in case of accident, and there are two to three weeks off work. Still, a finger is a finger, and it's a difficult decision for a man to make.

Wo-ow, wo-ow. Our parents are still in bed and I'm able to read a Mickey Spillane novel at the breakfast table. My sister Heather takes her time to cut her school-lunch. She is fourteen, an attractive and good-natured girl with a big bust which spreads the pleats of her gym frock. All she wants from life is to get married and have lots of children. For as long as we can remember she has been gathering names for babies: Violet and Pansy, Roland and Ruby, Hugh, Jimmy and Marigold.

Heather is not fond of school and thinks she might be getting a period pain.

'Take an A.P. Codeine,' I say from the pages of *I, the Jury*.

'I feel really awful.' She tries to look the part, hoping that I'll advise her to stay home from school. I ignore her and she goes through the hall to wake up Mum.

We-ow, we-ow, we-ow.

I have three sisters and a brother, all younger than I. Joan, a pretty girl with sandy hair and freckles, is a nurse aid at Kimberley Hospital, Levin. Then there is Heather. Next comes Barbara, a shy dark nine-year-old who has Dad's tendency to rheumatic fever. Five-year-old Peter is the youngest and looks most like me except for his orange hair and green eyes.

My mother's slippers sound down the hall. Mickey Spillane is quickly replaced by a textbook open at polysaccharides.

'Heather's staying home from school,' says Mum. 'She's got her monthlies.'

My sister catches my eye and says defensively, 'I'm not missing much. It's only sports.'

That explains everything. We all got sick on sports days. All the same, it's a wonder Mum doesn't remember that Heather had the same ailment two weeks ago.

We-ow. The stripping mill is a quarter of a mile away, yet its singing fills our house.

My mother has brought out the clock from the bedroom. 'Joy, you're going to be late for work. What's the matter with you? Been reading again? You'll get the sack, you will.'

It's true. I'm late, I'm late, under the mattress with Mickey Spillane, and out the door, buttoning my smock at the shoulder, onto my push-bike, blow, forgot to comb my hair, standing on the pedals, we-ow, we-ow, and now in front of me, the nine o'clock clamouring of the school bell.

I wouldn't be late if I had a motorbike.

We feel sorry for Mr Beaumont because his wife won't let him drink. She is very strict about it and has removed him from all temptation by shifting to Foxton Beach and selling the car. He sits marooned in a house as dry as the surrounding sand-dunes, doesn't go out except once a fortnight when she gives him a bus fare to come into Foxton and visit the doctor.

Mr Beaumont lives for that fortnightly visit. For thirteen days he is a dour man with a slack lower lip and a red face which runs downhill in lines of disappointment; but on the fourteenth day he glows like the sun and his eyes shine with recklessness.

He brings his prescription into the shop, wishing us all a truly good day. 'I'll be off now to pay my social calls, you understand,' he says, twirling his hat by the brim. 'I'd be greatly obliged if one of you young ladies would acquaint me of the bus time, as per usual.'

'Don't worry, Mr Beaumont. You can rely on us.'

'Ah, I knew I could. And that other little matter — if Mrs Beaumont should telephone — I'm still at the doctor's.' His wink is exaggerated.

'Of course, Mr Beaumont.'

We don't know where he gets the money. Perhaps he doesn't have any and relies on the generosity of his friends. Whatever, near time for the five-thirty bus back home, Mr Beaumont is as happy as you please, and none too steady.

I walk across the road to the hotel and push through the doors of the public bar. Cyril the barman waves a towel. 'Over there, the silly old bugger.'

Mr Beaumont is standing on a chair by the window, reciting a poem about a dog with a limitless bladder. When he sees me he swallows the rest of the verse and gets down off the chair. He sets his hat square on his head and draws a line with his eye to the door. 'Thankee, my dear,' he says. 'Much obliged.' Then he charges across the bar with determination, out and onto the street. I give him his prescription and a small bag of peppermints, and then help him to his bus. As I go back across the street, I wave to him, and he, now composed in his seat, doffs his hat in a tidy farewell.

Then comes the day when we forget.

It's time to close the shop and I'm picking up the mats in the dispensary, ready to sweep out. The bus grinds past the door and Marjorie gives a cry, 'Mr Beaumont!'

I let the mats go. 'Mr Beaumont.'

Mr Reddie looks at me and shakes his head. 'You'd better go over and see if he's still there. All else failing, I'll run him home when I've finished.'

I go to the hotel and push through the crowded bar. Mr Beaumont is asleep with his head on the bar near the till. Cyril mops up round him. 'I tried to tell him it was his bus time. Wouldn't believe me, the silly old drongo.'

I shake Mr Beaumont but he's as responsive as a large kapok mattress. 'Wake up, Mr Beaumont. You've missed your bus. Mr Beaumont? It's time to go home.'

Without lifting his head, he peers at me through watering eyes. '— take you home again, Kathleen,' he murmurs and goes back to sleep.

Artie Hines, from the service station, comes over, glass of beer in hand. 'Having trouble, eh? Not to worry. We just mended a tractor tyre, got to drop it off at the beach. We can give him a lift.'

'Would you really?'

'Too right. Got to get him home or that missus of his'll take the town apart. Hey, you fellahs, give us a hand, will you?'

Two men in grease-stained overalls came forward. They hook Mr Beaumont under the arms and drag him off his stool. Artie follows, carrying Mr Beaumont's hat, and I follow Artie. Outside there is a grey truck with tools and a tractor wheel on the back.

'He'll be good as gold up there,' says Artie. 'One, two, three, and up you go, my beauty.'

As Mr Beaumont bounces on to the back of the truck, he opens his eyes and smiles at us. Then, conducting with his hands over his chest, he sings, 'I'll take you home again, Kathleen, to where your heart will know no pain.'

For an old man with emphysema he sings remarkably well.

I give Artie Hines the prescription and explain what the peppermints are for.

'Bit too late for that, sin't it?' says Artie. 'He's dropped himself in the dunny, this time. Need more than peppermints, if you ask me.

'All right up there, my beauty? Don't you go falling off.'

Mr Beaumont waves grandly. 'Much obliged to you. Very kind. "And when the fields are fresh and green, I will take you to your home, Kathleen —" '

A moment later his voice is lost in the roar of a tattered muffler and the truck bears him away down the main street, his legs hanging over the edge of the tray, his hands still conducting his song.

'He'll be for it,' says a knowing bystander.

Mr Beaumont doesn't come into town again. His wife arranges for the doctor to make house-calls and all prescriptions are sent out on the bus. Four months later, Mr Beaumont dies in his sleep.

Cyril the barman, comes in to tell us the news. 'Poor old bugger,' he says and he is crying.

My parents' marriage is often stormy. Mum and Dad have the kind of romantic ideals which are portrayed on the cinema screen and which are all too fragile for the harsh realities of sickness and poverty and a large family. It is true that for some people, adversity builds character, but for many it is destructive and demeaning. My parents are not well-equipped to deal with hardship, and they suffer cruelly. But through the storms, the violence, the shouting and shrieking, their romance does survive to blossom suddenly and beautifully as soon as the climate improves.

In spite of my father's deafness, they get a lot of pleasure from singing together. My mother has a voice of unrealised greatness. In different circumstances she could have been an operatic mezzo-soprano on the world stage. As it is, she drowns the church choir in splendid sound and fills the street with 'Gypsy Love Song' or 'Rose Marie' while she is hanging out the washing.

My father's voice is pale by comparison but adequate, and on summer evenings they sit at the old harmonium and sing until they are hoarse. Dad's favourites are 'Annie Laurie', 'The Old Rugged Cross' and 'Whispering Hope'. He sings them very slowly and significantly while Mum fills out the harmony. Sometimes we children are called in to supplement with our thin, reedy voices; but none of us shows promise or enthusiasm. We are, after all, the generation of ready-made wireless music and this effort seems unnecessary. Besides, our parents' singing is not really a family affair — we sense that without understanding why. Their duets are part of some larger overture.

Sometimes they leave the harmonium and dance round the room, singing against each other with much affection. Then Dad stops and glares at us. 'Away to ye beds!' he orders. 'Ye'll be guid f'r nothing in the morning. Dinna stop their gawkin'. Did ye no hear what I said? Away wi' ye!'

On a cold winter evening, the family gathers round the coal-range in the kitchen. The oven door is open and inside are bricks which will later be put into socks to warm our beds. Our parents sit with their feet in the oven; this is their privilege. The rest of us take up positions round the stove on a first come, first served basis, and we sit reading, knitting, sewing, squabbling amongst ourselves in voices too low to attract a clout from either parent.

Dad begins to hum 'Abide With Me' and he reaches for Mum's hand. She joins in and before long they are singing for all they're worth and the kitchen is vibrating with the fullest notes. When the hymn is finished, Dad draws Mum across until she is sitting on his knee, then he says to us, 'I'll tell ye this for nothing — I wed the most beautiful girl in the whole wide world.'

I go on reading.

'None o'ye got a patch on her looks.' He puts his arms round her waist and jiggles her on his knee, singing, 'I love a lassy, a bony, bonny lassy —'

Mum laughs. Reluctantly I close my book.

We are not allowed to waste power by burning lights in our bedrooms, but if I depart now, I'll be able to snatch the torch unnoticed and read under the bedclothes. I take my brick from the oven and put it in a sock.

My father sings, 'She's as sweet as the heather, the bonny, purple heather —'

I pause at the pantry to lift the torch, and then go to my bedroom, arching my feet over the iciness of the lino. Book and torch go under the pillow, the brick is put at the bottom of the bed.

Through the wall, I hear my father say, 'Time the rest of ye went tae y'r byes. Off and away wi' ye.'

And my mother says, 'You heard your father, didn't you? Do what you're told — this minute!'


There is a rule that we may not have boyfriends until we are eighteen. Joan and Heather consider this most unfair, especially since our mother was married at eighteen, and I suspect from their giggles and whispers, and from the smell of cigarette smoke on their clothing, that their social experience goes beyond the permitted Bible Class picnics and dances. I am greatly concerned for my sisters, and more than a little envious. The restriction on boyfriends suits me because it gives me an excuse for being out of the pairing game. In truth, I am convinced that no interesting boy would look twice at me. Why should he? I don't dress well. I don't know how to dance. Attempts at dancing have ended in failure: boys tell me I insist on leading. I don't know what they mean by that and I don't care. Dancing seems to me to be a futile exercise.

I am not without experience of boys. I have been kissed three times: outside the school gates when I was eleven; once at sixteen in the back of a car; and in a darkened street one night after church.

The most attractive thing about kissing, is remembering it afterwards. When it's happening there are practical concerns which prevent enjoyment; getting noses in the way, trying to breathe, avoiding the clashing of teeth, wondering about tongues and spit and germs. But somewhere in the kiss there is a pleasure which becomes apparent afterwards, a small excitement which grows in solitude until it becomes detached from the other partner and exists for its own sake.

I haven't had a boyfriend according to my parents' definition, but I have been in and out of love since the age of four. Love is the condition which makes, shapes and colours my life; it is also its greatest weakness. Love is all misery, all bliss. Love is the inspiration behind nearly everything I learn and achieve. Love is a pain. Love is enervating. Without it, I feel desperate.

Often, love has been associated with some living person, adoration at a distance of favourite uncles, a standard five teacher, film actors Leslie Howard and Mel Ferrer. Sometimes the attachment has been to the character in a novel, sometimes to a long-dead author or artist. I have been smitten by Frederic Chopin and Robert Louis Stevenson. Van Gogh would not have committed suicide if he had known me. As for John Keats, well, there is the great love of my life. I have remained faithful to him for two and a half years and I read his works as often as I read the Bible. I press flowers between the pages of his poems. Sometimes I write out verses and burn them with dried rose petals in a little crockery dish at the back of the garden. I feed upon his melancholy.

*Yes, I will be thy priest and build a fane*
*In some untrodden region of the mind,*
*Where branched thoughts, new grown with pleasant pain*
*Instead of pines shall murmur in the wind.*

This love I feel has nothing to do with sexual restlessness and that other business of making babies. Rather, it seems to make itself felt above the waist. The head is full of it, as are the eyes, ears and mouth. It burns in the palms of the hands and is a weakness between the shoulder blades. It is a stammering of the heart, an aching in the lungs; but its true kingdom lies fair and square in the stomach. When love enters, it leaves a hole in the solar pelux so wide that the whole world seems to pass through after it.

Love is such a frequent visitor that it now thinks it owns me and it will arrive without invitation. It can be enough to see raindrops on a leaf or to observe the perfect dappling of colour on a cat's fur, to feel the beginnings of the yawning and yearning under the ribs.

Some nights, all too rarely, there is a marvellous dream which is filled with an emotion not experienced in waking. I am standing on a cliff above the sea. Behind me there are the white columns of a temple; in front there is blueness, blue sky down to blue sea. I drive from the cliff and discover there is no skin between sky and sea; one element diffuses into the other. As I enter the richer blueness of the water, I see that the bottom of the ocean is covered with white marble paving-stones, and there are white pillars similar to those on top of the cliff. I breathe easily as I swim between the pillars, looking for a marble staircase. My heart beats with an eager pain, for I know that when I find the staircase, I shall also find the man. Patches of light and shade shimmer on the whiteness which extends to tunnels to columns and arches, and my breath goes before me in silver bubbles.

Then I see the staircase and my chest aches with sweetness, for there is the man coming down the steps to meet me. His hands are outstretched and he smiles with such pleasure that clearly he has been waiting for me since the last dream. He is all gold. His hair floats golden behind him, his skin is like polished metal. He swims with haste, reaches for me, then we are side by side, arms round each other, hips and legs touching. We float like that — like two people in a three-legged race. Gradually, his body passes into mine. He is absorbed through my side until he is totally within me, shining gold through my skin. In that moment of extraordinary pleasure, I am the man and he is also me.

I awake feeling golden and contented. I do not know enough to ask myself what the dream means.

Occasionally on a pale frost day, I will buy a lunch of hot pie and go down to the Foxton wharf where the river unwinds sluggishly against ice-encrusted piles. It's a good place for eels. They can be caught by the dozen, green-fleshed monsters made inedible by their diet of flax strippings, but good for garden fertiliser. When I was younger, dad and I used to come here on a dark night and catch them by the trailer-load.

Sometimes I take my pie across the railway lines and chat with Harvey who sits in his doll's house of a station waiting for the daily 'whitebait express'. The train comes at irregular times, and so slowly that if you are further up the track you are welcome to jump up on the footplate and ride into the station with the driver and fireman.

They say the whitebait express has a record unequalled anywhere in the world: it has never been on time. The story goes that one day the whistle was heard a few seconds before the hour written up on the timetable. No one could believe it. Local shopkeepers whipped a hat around and rushed down to the station to congratulate the driver. For the first time in history, the train had come in on time.

'Hold your horses, boys,' said the driver. 'This, here, is yesterday's train.'

One train a day is not sufficient to keep the track clear of weeds. In spring the rails are flanked with buttercups, clover, pink oxalis, dandelions and shivery grass. In the area between the station and the wharf, the grass and lupins grow waist high and often of a morning you see Mrs Schmidt with her sack, fossicking amongst the weeds for discarded beer bottles. She wears old tennis shoes and rolled down stockings and as she walks she mutters to herself in German. She is still bitter about the defeat of her country nine years ago, but is in no way to blame for it. Her own war effort was courageous and unrelenting and consisted of lying in the long grass outside her house, throwing stones at passing cars.

Foxton is one of those towns which absorbs people without question or comment. In years to come I will learn about social acceptability and the need to conform to certain behavioural patterns, but there is none of that here. No one is surprised that Maria Schmidt threw stones at cars or that Mr Howell wears pages of the Bible in his shoes to stop the forces of evil coming up from hell through the soles of his feet.

Miss Sylvia Glover believes that my boss is poisoning her. She sends samples of her phenobarb mixture to the Health Department for analysis and has also written to the New Zealand Railways Road Services demanding that they reroute their buses which go past her house. She says that every time a bus goes past, her mouth hurts.

Mr Pitihana is a small thin man who used to be a jockey. He can eat 14 dozen raw oysters without swallowing once.

Mrs Stephenson often calls at the pharmacy. She is a sweet, frail lady in her eighties. She has a glowing smile and always carries a covered wicker-basket. While we are making up her prescription, she works quickly, filling her basket with goodies: perfume, face cream, lipsticks, films, laxatives, aspirin, cottonwool. When she leaves, Mr Reddie phones her daughter who cries, 'Oh no, not again.'

The daughter returns the goods the same afternoon.

My boss says soothingly, 'Can't be helped, I suppose. Age comes to us all.'

'Age, my foot!' says the daughter. 'Have you been inside our house? Just count the number of things that are handbag size. She's been at it all her life.'

Peter Pojursky comes to town in his horse-drawn dray and insists that motor cars will go out of fashion. His horse is a lumbering thing with tasselled feet and a small beard under its chin. The women come out with fire shovels to collect its droppings for their gardens.

Then there is Mr Roach who doesn't hold with paper money. He collects his pension in silver and copper which he carries in a woman's shoulder-bag made of alligator skin.

Mrs Waaka is proud of her nephew who sings. Once she brought him along to the school and he sang for us 'Little Fellow with his Mammy's Eyes'. Now he's in London and she comes into the shop to tell us of his latest success. His name is Inia Te Wiata.

I sit on the edge of the wharf, finish my pie and brush the crumbs off my smock. The Post Office Savings Bank book in the pocket is waiting to receive my pay and is still desperately short of the amount needed for a deposit on a bike.

Harvey, the station-master, knows about my ambition.

'Why don't you get a James?' he says. 'That's about the right size for you. A little James Captain, hundred and ninety-odd ccs.'

'I'm saving for a Gold Flash.'

'Bit on the heavy side for a girl.'

'Nope,' I say. 'I can handle it.'

And I go back to the dispensary to cod liver oil, ointments, penciller lozenges, and dreams of speed.

Boyfriends are one thing. Friends, who are male, are another. I have a number of the latter, ranging in age from eight to 76, but there is a small group in their late teens whom I cultivate with shameless assiduity. These, of course, are the owners of motorbikes.

My parents — with that uncanny knowing which parents have — realise that there is no 'nonsense' about these friendships and I am free to go down to George's or Allen's on a Saturday afternoon and mess about with bikes.

The boys are accommodating. If I help them to clean their machines, to sand down frames ready for painting, rinse out chains in petrol, vulcanise tubes, clean carburettors, cut out new gaskets, then I can have the occasional ride. Once I got an A.J.S. for a whole afternoon. The boys were having races on Foxton beach. I was given a bike and left at the fork of the road to watch for traffic cops. If a patrol car took one turning towards the beach, I was to race down the other and warn the boys. But the reckless ride was not to be. There was no sign of the law and I sat at the fork for more than three hours before I was released from sentry duty.

Allen is 18 and has compulsory military training coming up. He has hinted that I might be able to look after his bike while he's in camp at Linton. I cling to the hope but there is now a problem. Allen has a girlfriend who disapproves of me. While we're working in the garage, she watches from the doorway, talking to Allen and giving me some very cold looks. She has told Allen she doesn't want me going round there any more.

I can still visit George but his bike is an old Indian, not far off the junk heap. It's a battle for me to get it off the rest and with all that compression, I usually end up standing on top of the kick-start, like an idiot.

It's Allen's machine I want. I bend scruples and add to my prayers the earnest plea that Allen will get rid of his girlfriend before he goes into army camp.

God is important in my life although I think there's a bit of conflict in our understanding of each other.

I teach Sunday School in the Presbyterian church, mainly because I enjoy telling children stories, and the Bible is full of rich dramatic narrative. On Sunday mornings I also attend Bible Class, and again I'm not slow in showing off how much I know of the Bible. But there's more to it than that. There's a satisfaction which can't be described, and it's especially there in the regular Sunday evening church service. I love the old building, the smell of aged wood and quiet of it, the flowers, the organ, the people who sit in the same places each week, like paintings on a wall — I love everything about church except the sermons. Sermons belong to that part of God which makes me uneasy: God the vengeful, God the Old Testament school-master, God of the shalt and shalt not. All that serious stuff worries me because it seems dishonest, God playing at being tough when he's just about splitting his sides. Because that's how he is outside of sermons. He laughs a lot. He created the universe in a gust of laughter and he's been amused ever since. Sometimes you can actually see all that mirth shaking in the sunlight.

God can also be very romantic and gentle. Sometimes I go off on my own to be with him, walking by the river, or sitting in the church when it's empty of all but light and flowers, and I think I know him well enough to be straight with him. This hell place, for example. I want to know if it's true, and if it is, well, it's just not fair, is it? And why did he give his son such a hard time? You'd think that being God he could fix up the sin business any way he wanted to.

Once in a while, I make a fourth observance of a Sunday and go to the Salvation Army hall in the afternoon. That's the place where they measure the laughter. There is a word for it. Jubilation. It's all about mountains skipping like oxen and rivers clapping their hands. I understand that. But I also need the other, the knowledge of pain and darkness, the tears of the suffering Christ.

Until I can resolve this duality, I will continue to worship God in two churches.


Because the pharmacy is the only one in town, it must offer a twenty-four-hour service. I can earn extra for my bike by looking after the dispensary while my boss is away for an evening. This mainly involves answering the door for prescriptions and spending the rest of the time in study. I may also do my chemistry experiments providing they don't leave residual odours of rotten eggs.

One night I open the side-door and see there a man who could have stumbled directly out of the graveyard in *Great Expectations*. He has been cut and bruised about the face, has startled eyes and is shaking. He stares about the dispensary. He is just out of prison, he says, and his nerves are very bad. Will I give him something to make him sleep?

I explain that I cannot do that.

He snatches up a bottle of Digoxin. What about these?

I tell him that they are for heart disease. Then I suggest that he goes to the doctor and gets a prescription.

No, no, no. He grasps the edge of the dispensary bench to still his hands, and tells me to phone the doctor. Now, he says. Phone now. And he pushes me to the phone on the wall.

He watches closely while I make the call.

The doctor's voice is measured and careful. He says that he will come at once, but in the meantime I am to give the man a script for seven nembutal.

I count the capsules into a phial and ask the man to sign a prescription while I type the label. 'The doctor's coming to see you,' I say.

Without a word, the man takes the top off the pill phial, tips all the capsules into his mouth and throws the empty container on the floor. He grabs the stock bottle of nembutal, pushes it into his pocket and stumbles out into the night.

When the doctor arrives, I am distraught, believing that the man intends to kill himself. The doctor shakes his head and tells me a little about drug addiction. There are many like that, he says.

I am appalled to learn that the means of healing can itself cause illness. Is there nothing purely good? I go home, somehow feeling responsible for a tattered man with panic in his eyes.

I have a number of casual evening and weekend jobs. Over the months, I do baby-sitting and house-cleaning. I take photographs at local functions, pluck and clean hens at a poultry farm, sell lupin seed to the catchment board, and mushrooms and blackberries to local people. On race-days I'm an extra waitress at the local grill-room. Regularly on a Saturday, I go to the rubbish tip with my father to scavenge for sacks and bottles, copper, lead and brass. My earnings over these months are handsome for one my age, and yet my savings barely grow. My parents are right. I am not good with money. My dreams of a bike are threatened by numerous extravagances: books mainly, photography gear, chocolates, materials for drawing and painting, a microscope and, most recently, subscriptions to two motorcycle magazines. I am constantly disgusted at my lack of thrift.

One afternoon, in September, my father comes into the pharmacy wearing the widest of grins. I've never seen him so pleased with himself.

'I've got ye a bike,' he announces.

I come out from behind the counter. He's not joking. He means it. He's bought me a motorbike.

'Ye can pay me back,' he says. 'It wasna cheap, mind you. Near on sixty quid.'

Sixty pounds? George's old Indian is worth more than that.

Dad leads me out of the shop and proudly indicates a machine propped against the kerb. It's a toy! It's a little old toy! He's bought a Royal Enfield 147cc with a hand gear change aligned against the petrol tank and a rubber bulb hooter.

I can't ride a thing like that!

He yanks it off the stand and kicks it over. It comes to life with a high-pitched cackle.

My eyes fill with tears.

'Aye, I'd knew ye'd like it,' says Dad.

After work, I take the bike round to Allen's place. 'It's only temporary,' I tell him. 'Something to get me from A to B while I'm saving up for a decent bike.'

Allen folds up with laughter. 'You look as though you're running on a couple of castors!'

I ride off in a sulk.

It's a rotten little bike and I hate it. The humiliation of puttering round on the half-grown machine drives me into a deep misery. I try to conceal my feelings from my father. He truly believes that he has made all my dreams come true.

On Saturday I put on a heavy coat and gloves, wind a scarf round my neck, fit on a pair of old flying goggles, and ride out of Foxton. It's not much of a bike but I might as well try it out on a longer run.

The engine goes into a high-pitched scream as I open up the throttle on the Himatangi straight. I let go of the handlebars and rock the tank with my knees, feeling the bike respond with one gentle arc after another. It does sixty-five flat out. My hair flaps like a rag, my cheeks blow out, water streams back from my eyes under the goggles, my knuckles freeze on the throttle. The wind in my face is so sharp I imagine it to be peeling the skin off. I put my head back and give a long yodelling cry which scarcely rises above the racing engine.

'Oh-ee-oh-ee-oh-ee-oh-ee-oh-ee-oh-ee-oh!'

In that moment the road rises under the wheels, the trees fling back their arms and the whole world shouts with laughter.

# FLOWERS

Mum reckoned that she couldn't face Gran at that hour of the morning, so while she got breakfast we took Gran her tea and a slice of bread and butter the way she liked it. Usually it was on the rosebud plate. Gran had a thing about flowers.

On that particular day she was wide awake and waiting, her teeth in and her hair spread out on the pillow like combed fleece. Her good eye had a sparkle in it as she said, 'You're lucky to be seeing me this morning.'

We made a space on the bed-table for the cup and saucer.

'I was near enough to gone last night.'

'Gone where, Gran?' said Margaret, giving me a knowing look.

'Just gone. Popped off.' Gran laughed. 'I tell you, it came on real bad in the night. I couldn't move an inch. And I thought, now here's a right old pickle, me off to meet the Almighty and I can't even reach me teeth. You sugar that tea?'

'Yes, Gran.'

'I mean sugar. None of those chemical things.'

'Sugar, Gran.'

'Ah, I don't know why your mother's trying to poison me. She'll be rid of me soon enough.'

'Gran, the doctor said you had to lose weight.'

'That's what she says, I'm sure, but the good Lord knows the truth of it.' She reached for her tea, and the cup rattled against the saucer. She sipped, made a rapid sucking sound, then smiled. 'Sugar, it is. You're fine girls, both of you, to your poor old Gran. You'll be having your reward in Heaven.'

'What are you going on about now?' It was Mum. She was standing in the doorway, her arms folded and her face all sharp for a fight.

Gran said to us, 'Go on — tell her.'

We looked away. We didn't want to get caught in one of these arguments.

'Tell her how I nearly popped off in the night. That's what she wants to hear. Good riddance to bad rubbish, she'll say.'

'Mother, I warned you!'

Gran picked up a piece of bread, folded it over, and pushed it into her mouth.

'Come on, you two,' Mum said to us. 'You were told to bring in her tea, not to stay for a committee meeting. Your breakfast is on the table getting cold.'

Gran's good eye winked at us. 'Take no notice. She always did have a fearful temper, even as a girl.'

At the table Mum said to Dad, 'Jim, she's driving me round the bend.'

Dad was sympathetic. 'You need a break. Why don't you go away this weekend? The girls and I can manage.'

'That's not going to solve anything. It's deliberate, Jim. She knows exactly how to get at me, and she's worse now than ever.'

Dad mumbled something about old age and hardening of the arteries. 'It makes her irritable,' he said.

'Irritable, my foot!' Mum replied. 'It's just plain nastiness. She enjoys it. You should have heard the way she was talking to the girls this morning.'

Dad patted her arm. We'll probably be the same one day, if that's any consolation.'

It wasn't.

'Never! I'd jump over a cliff before I got like her.'

'Perhaps she needs an interest,' said Dad, persistently helpful.

'She's got her crochet. She watches television.'

'I mean an outdoor interest. She's still reasonably mobile. Some sort of exercise.'

'Brilliant!' said Mum. 'Every eighty-year-old who's had a stroke should take up jogging.'

'I was thinking of something more in the line of gardening,' said Dad.

'Gardening?' Mum was stilled.

'She was always keen on gardening. Why don't you give her one of your flower beds to look after?'

Margaret and I looked at each other. We had often thought that the trouble between Mum and Gran came from the fact that they were so alike, even down to their love of flowers. Mum kept the flower beds in front of the house like pictures from a gardening book, and too bad for any cat or dog that strayed onto them. No one, not even Margaret or I was allowed to touch her flowers.

Mum sat without saying a word.

'It would be a nice gesture,' said Dad, looking at her and understanding. 'It won't be for ever,' he said.

'I'll think about it,' Mum said.

We all knew what it cost her to give up the bed by the mail box. It was the smallest of the flower beds but the prettiest with tall blue delphiniums in the centre, then a ring of pink and red phlox and verbena, some frilled snapdragons, and an outer circle of pansies — brown, purple, yellow.

We could see that Gran was touched. She hobbled out there with her stick and got down on her knees to smell the verbena.

'It's me own garden,' she said, peering up at Mum.

'Yes, mother.'

'And you mean that? You'll not be interfering?'

'I told you. It's yours.'

Gran picked a pansy and tucked it into her shawl. 'It'll be nice having a garden again.'

A few days later Mum had to go out for the afternoon. She came home to find that every flower had been pulled out of the garden by the mail box. In the bare earth stood two dozen pale green seedlings with stiff leaves.

'Cabbages,' said Gran. 'I planted some cabbages.'

When Dad got in from work, Mum was sitting at the table crying. He sat beside her, his arm round her shoulders, and tried to comfort her.

'I can't take any more, Jim,' she wept. 'That's final. She's got to go into a home.'

'I'll talk to her,' he said.

'It's no good. I've already told her. I said straight out I can't stand it any longer and she has to go.'

Margaret and I thought that Gran had gone too far, but we didn't like to say anything. The truth was we loved both Mum and Gran, and we hated having to take sides.

It was Gran who brought up the subject. She said to us, 'Well, I'll not be with you much longer, my dears. You've heard, have you? Herself is putting me in the poor house.'

We didn't answer.

'Putting me on the rubbish heap, she is. I always knew she wanted to get rid of me.'

Margaret said, 'You shouldn't have done that to the garden, Gran. Mum loved those flowers.'

'It was me own garden.'

'You — you planted cabbages!' I said.

'And what's wrong with God's own cabbages?' she demanded.

Mum and Dad went out to dinner that night. In the morning there was still a tight feeling in the air, but no one spoke again of Gran going into a home. Gran was careful not to make Mum mad, and when we went out to the gate we tried not to look at the garden near the mail box.

It was only a couple of weeks after, that Gran had another stroke. She died in the ambulance on the way to hospital.

Margaret and I couldn't get used to the idea that she had gone. She had talked about it so often that we thought it would never happen. Her room looked the same as always, with her crocheted bedspread, her reading glasses, her holy pictures, her hairbrush and hairnets and her bottles of pills. Even the smell of her was there. It was as though she had left for a day or two.

The strange thing was, it was Mum who was hit the hardest. Her face was swollen with crying, and she spoke about Gran as though they'd never quarrelled in all their years together. When the friends and relations came back to the house from the cemetery, Mum talked non-stop about what a wonderful woman her mother was, all the outstanding things she'd done in her life, her charity work, her gardening, how she used to win silver cups for the roses she grew. Then she told the story about the cabbages, making it sound so funny that everybody laughed thinking what a character Gran was right to the end.

The other strange thing was that Mum didn't pull out those cabbages. She weeded round them, and as they began to heart she picked off the caterpillars.

'Aren't you going to plant flowers?' Margaret said.

Mum went on weeding as though she hadn't heard. After a bit she looked up at us in a vague sort of way, and asked had we ever noticed how much cabbages looked like roses.

# THE CLEANING
# OF WINDOWS

When he cut down the tree she came flapping at him like a ship in full sail, hair flying, arms tilting. He'd never seen her so mad.

'It's only an old manuka,' he said, trying to match his voice to hers. 'Gee, Aunty Magda, you said good burning wood.'

'I said driftwood!' she roared. 'There's plenty along the beach!'

'Some of it's water-logged. It's full of salt. It'll burn your chimney out.'

'Thank you, Sam, but I've been burning driftwood for forty years. I haven't lost a chimney yet, or a good healthy tree. What got into your skull?'

'I read it somewhere. You're not supposed to burn wood that's been in the sea.'

She crouched right down to touch the edge of the manuka stump. He saw the way she wiped her hand across the wet red wood and he thought, she can take a running jump, the silly old chook.

She looked up at him. 'Your trouble, Sam, is you believe every flipping thing you're told. Open your eyes, boy. Think for yourself. You got to in that house of yours or you'll end up with your brain in a matchbox.' She stood up slowly, her hands in the middle of her back. 'Get in the habit of questioning bloody everything.'

'But it's common sense, Aunty Magda. The salts in the driftwood burn hotter —'

'Salts, my backside! Get out the tractor and go down to the beach. I'll give you a hand.'

Strong with anger, he went into the shed, took the battery off the charger and carried it in his arms to the old David Brown. Like everything else on the farm, the tractor ran on patches. The wiring was bandaged with sticking plaster, strips of plastic shopping bags and bits of sacking. A hole in the inlet manifold had a jam jar lid glued on it. A cracked head meant that the engine could only be run cold but it went all right. Like her, it was a bit rusty but it still had a lot of go.

While he was connecting the battery, she came and heaved the trailer on to the drawbar and then she got up and stood there in her gumboots and brown coat done up with safety pins. He didn't look except from the edge of his eye but he could feel her stare on him, waiting for him to do one more thing wrong.

He knew what he was about and he showed her, firing up the old David Brown and swinging the trailer in a wide arc through the gateway and down the track to the beach. Only when he hit the rough patch did he look back. She was still standing on the trailer, hands on hips, grey hair bouncing out of the woollen cap, still trying to stare him out. His father was right. She was as crazy as a cock-eyed cow.

He stopped the tractor down the beach a bit and she helped him gather up the grey bones of trees which had been stacked along the stones by flood tides, some of them wet and too heavy to move, some laced up with kelp. It was hard work. They didn't talk much until the trailer was near enough to loaded and she needed a rest. Then, leaning back against the tractor wheel, she pointed across the bay.

'Sam, you ever notice something about those hills? They're

all female.'

He shaded his eyes with his hand. The sea was as flat as green oil except for patches fired by the sun. The land was the same as always, dark green bush to the water's edge, a few birds flying, a couple of holiday baches white in the distance, a yacht moored off Weka Point.

'Every bit of land in the Marlborough Sounds,' she said. 'Thighs, shoulders, breasts and bellies, all ways you look. See? There and there? Shapes of women —'

He looked and looked away again.

'— lying in the water. Look at the crease in that bottom. Look at the elbow raised like she was pushing herself out of the sea.'

'Yeah,' he said, uncoiling the rope from under the trailer.

'You ever notice that before, Sam?'

'No.'

'You see it now?'

'Yeah. Kind of.' He threw the rope over the trailer and looked back over his shoulder at the hills squatting on their own reflections. 'I suppose they're lady shapes, all right.'

'All wrong!' She pounced on him, jabbing her finger at his chest. 'They're just hills. That's all. The rest I made up. See what I mean, Sam boy? You got to look at things the way they are. Don't just take anybody's old say-so. Those aren't women. Those aren't any nonsense excepting hills.'

'I know that,' he said, but it was already too late. The mask of the hills had been removed showing the contours he had seen on forbidden late movies. The shapes shifted as he looked and dared him to possess them by giving them names. He licked his top lip, pulled the rope tight and knotted it, tested the tension to make sure the wood couldn't slide off, and all the while his eyes were furtively touching hollows thick with manuka scrub and peaks tilted up to the sun. 'I know they're just hills,' he said, hating her.

No matter what he felt at times, or what was said at home, he didn't like other people talking about her. When the kids at school called her names, he could do something about it. He was bigger than they were. But with adults it was different.

The day the new dental nurse came, he was sitting outside the staff room eating his lunch when through the window, clear as a bell, came Mr Pruitt's voice. 'It's a queer set-up. Brother and sister can't stand each other. Never could I'm told. The farm was left to them both but they cut it in two. Harry's got one side of the peninsula, Magdalena, the other. There's an eight foot high deer fence running along the spur of the hill between the two properties, real Colditz stuff. The brother farms his side but hers has gone back to bush, a pity really. She's as mad as a meat axe and just as tough. Spends most of her time out fishing.'

For as long as he could remember, her back porch had been littered with useless things, broken machinery, burnt-out toasters and irons, knives without handles, sick hens, orphaned lambs. A one-legged pukeko lived there. She fed it every day because it couldn't scratch for a living, she said. At night the possums came in to eat the leftovers. He had learned to watch where he put his feet.

He took his gumboots into the wash-house and in the cool dark he turned on a tap to wash his hands. The window had been broken and sealed with cardboard so that only a rim of light shone past the cobwebs and dead blowflies. It was a while before he saw that the tub under the tap was already half-full of water and in it was a large drowned crayfish.

'Gee, that's big!' he yelled.

'Lunch!' she called back.

'Where'd you get it?'

'In one of the cray pots.'

'Yeah, but where?'

She came into the wash-house and lifted the crayfish from the tub. Her hand was fair stretched to hold it. 'I found me a new spot at the back of the Chetwodes. You know the reef where we get the big cod? Half a chain north of that.'

'What's a chain in metres?'

'How would I know? No one asked me if the country could go metric. That's dead enough. I can't abide the cruelty of dropping living creatures into boiling water. Come on, wash your hands.'

Still in her coat and woollen cap, she stoked up the wood stove and filled the big preserving pan. 'It's a bit deep out there. That's why the divers have missed it, I reckon. Must be dozens of the beasties. You cut us some bread, eh? This is the fourth big one in three days. Think you can manage half?'

They ate the hot crayfish with butter, salt and pepper, sucking the meat out of the legs and scooping out the coral with their fingers. Afterwards, he offered to wash the dishes.

But she'd got up from the table and was settling herself in the big chair. 'You don't get paid for doing dishes,' she said, putting a cushion on the wooden box. She took off her woollen socks, one grey, one brown, while he poured olive oil from a bottle into a tin mug.

'Your hands warm?' she said.

'Warm enough.' He sat on the floor beside her and she put her feet up on the box.

'I might go to sleep before the hour is up but don't stop,' she said. 'If you hear me snore just go gentle like.'

He tipped oil into the palm of his hand and allowed it to warm there.

'You'll get five bucks today.'

'Five!'

'The rate's going up because you're good.' She closed her eyes. 'But you get nothing for cutting down that poor bloody tree,' she said.

'What do you do over there?' his mother asked.

'Oh — things.'

'What sort of things?'

'All sorts.' He gave his dinner full attention but she wasn't going away.

'Like what?'

Now his father was focused too. He had eyes the same colour as Aunty Magda's, a sort of washed-out grey.

'Like —' He noticed that on the bench there was a bit of scrunched up newspaper which his mother had used for cleaning the kitchen windows. 'I clean windows for her.'

His mother's mouth opened but it was a while before the laugh came. 'Magda clean windows?'

He shook his head. 'Uh-uh. I told you. She gets me to do them.'

'Harry, did you hear that? She's getting Sam to do her housework, for heaven's sake!'

'What's she paying you?' his father asked.

'Three dollars an hour.'

'Three? So who's complaining? Listen, when I was his age I'd have shovelled shit with my mouth for three bucks an hour.'

'She's never cleaned windows,' his mother said. 'Why should she start now?'

'Maybe she likes to see out. I dunno. Five bucks is five bucks, eh Sam?'

'Yeah.' He laughed.

'How do you clean them?' his mother asked.

'Newspaper. I rub them with wet newspaper and then with dry.'

'Well, all I can say is it's a pity you don't get in some practice at home,' she replied.

'You don't give him the right incentive,' his father laughed, rubbing his thumb and forefinger together.

'What else do you do over there?' his mother asked.

'We had crayfish for lunch,' he said. 'It was huge.'

'You're kidding!' His father leaned forward. 'A real packhorse?'

'Just about. Aunty Magda's found a new place for her cray pots. She says there are hundreds.'

'Where?'

'Back of the Chetwodes. That place I showed you where we get the big cod — a bit north of there. How far is half a chain?'

'About here to the clothesline. Is she still setting her pots?'

'Every night. It's deep. She says the divers have missed it.' Then he caught the shine in his father's eyes and said, 'You can't set any pots in her place, Dad.'

His father laughed. 'Don't worry. I wouldn't dream of it.'

Aunty Magda had long cold feet as hard as boards, white in the middle and yellow where the skin was thick. He knew her feet so well that he could have drawn maps of them with his eyes closed. In fact, anytime he shut his eyes he could see them, the toes which curled under nails as thick as sheep's hooves, the flat plains criss-crossed by lines, the dry cracked areas of the heels, the bumps and lumps along the sides. He wondered if people ever read fortunes from the soles of feet.

When he'd warmed the oil, he'd spread it over the entire foot, then, with one hand under her heel and the other round her toes, he'd move the foot in circles to loosen her ankle joint. That made her relax, she said. Next would come the toes, one at a time, rubbing and squeezing each cold little hill of flesh, and massaging down into the valleys which separated them.

He couldn't bear to have anyone touch the soles of his feet. When he was a little kid and his mother had tried to wash the soles of his feet in the bath, he'd squirmed out of control, his head going back under the water.

Aunty Magda didn't move. He could tickle, he could scratch, he could press his fingernails into the skin until they left marks but her feet stayed dead still. Her head was still too, resting back on the chair, eyes closed, although sometimes she'd moan softly down her nose.

While she was taking off her socks, she said, 'You didn't tell your father about my crayfish possie.'

He shrugged the question away.

'Did you?'

'Did I what?'

'Tell your father where I'm getting crays?'

'No, of course I didn't.' He felt bad about lying.

'Good. This is one thing he's not getting his thieving hands on.'

He poured the oil into the mug. 'Aunty Magda, why can't you and Dad be friends?'

'Friends?' She looked surprised. Then she lay back in the chair. 'Too much blood under the bridge.'

'What do you mean?'

'You don't get paid for asking questions,' she said.

He heard his parents talking in bed, his mother saying, 'I don't like him going over there every week.'

'It doesn't do any harm.'

'Don't be so sure. She's got a strong influence on him.'

'Sam's a sensible kid.'

'He's only twelve. She fills his head with nutty ideas.'

'Yeah, yeah, but he knows they're nutty. Look, you should encourage him. One day she's going to leave him that farm. She's got no one else to leave it to.'

At school, Miss Tolley had them out in the football paddock, drawing pictures of trees and the bike shed.

Craig did some drawings which set the kids laughing and when Miss Tolley asked to see, he screwed the paper up and shoved it in his pocket. She made him take it out and show her the pictures.

Craig protested, 'It wasn't my idea, Miss Tolley. It was Sam. He reckoned hills are tits.'

The other kids laughed and yelled.

Miss Tolley turned her head. 'Did you say that, Sam?'

He didn't answer. His face was hot as fire.

'I'm very disappointed, Sam,' Miss Tolley said.

Some of the others were adding fire to his burning. 'He said bums, too, Miss Tolley. Some hills are bums and some are tits.'

Miss Tolley sighed. 'To the impure all things are impure. You may go inside, Sam, and work at your desk.'

He woke suddenly, some time before light, hearing the scrape of the dinghy on the beach outside his window. He couldn't see anything for the garden trees, but in a while he heard the splash of oars and then the sound of a diesel engine. On the dark grey water, the black shape of his father's boat moved, without lights, beyond the trees and disappeared round the point.

He went into his parents' room and switched on the light. 'Where's Dad going?' he asked his mother.

'Mum?'

She rolled over, flinging her arm across the empty space in the bed.

'What's Dad doing with the boat?'

'Sam, for goodness sake! It's only half past four!'

'I heard Dad go out in the boat.'

'He's putting out a set line. Go back to bed.'

'Why didn't he wake me?'

'You've got school. Please, Sam! Put out the light. It's killing me!'

When he came home that afternoon, he discovered that his father had gone to town. He'd got a case of snapper, his mother said, and he'd taken them into the restaurant.

'Snapper? How big?'

'Oh, so-so.'

'Where'd he get them?'

'Beatrix Bay. He said they're running well.'

'That's good.'

But he immediately went out to look in the back of the garage. He saw that his father's diving gear was dry in the cupboard and hanging from the rafters were the cray pots, strung with cobwebs and dust.

On Sunday morning he helped her set up the smokehouse for six silver belly eels.

The smokehouse was an old fridge with the bottom knocked out, planted up the hill by the back of the house. There was a chimney dug in the earth and covered with sheets of iron, a hole for a fire at the other end.

While he hung the salted eels on hooks, she lit the fire. He noticed that she was using twigs from the manuka tree he'd cut down but he didn't say anything. He closed the smokehouse door. 'Dad's been catching a lot of snapper lately. You been getting any?'

'No. Is he smoking them?'

'Uh-uh. Takes them to a restaurant in town. Only we're not supposed to say, because he hasn't got a licence.'

'What restaurant?'

'I don't know.'

She blew on the fire. The twigs flared and crackled. 'It's nice someone's lucky. I haven't had a cray all week. Think I might just have a poacher.' She threw a handful of sawdust over the flames. 'You sure you didn't tell your father about my possie?'

'He hasn't been near it. He puts his lines out in Beatrix Bay.'

'So you did tell him.'

'I think —' He struggled. 'I don't remember. I might of.'

She was looking at him, waiting for more.

'It definitely isn't Dad. I looked. His cray pots are hanging in the shed, all dusty. Maybe there just aren't any more crayfish there.'

'Maybe so.' She got up slowly, unwinding her back. 'You're a good boy, Sam. Dopey but worthy.' She put her hand on his head. 'You should hear the way my feet talk about you.'

He woke up suddenly Monday morning, thinking the house was on fire. Why fire, he didn't know, except that his mother had set off screaming like that once before when a pan of fat had gone up in flames.

'Oh my God oh my God!'

He stumbled and bumped down the hall and into the kitchen doorway. It was his father who was hurt. He was sitting in a chair near the table and he had tea-towels wrapped round both his hands like huge red-soaked boxing gloves. His face was white as bone and there was blood everywhere, on the floor, on Mum's night-gown, on the table, blood dripping down his wet fishing clothes.

His mother was yelling, 'My God, Harry! I've got to get you to a hospital!'

They left him to get ready for school on his own, but he didn't. He went down to the beach, launched the blood-spattered dinghy and rowed round the point to Aunt Magda's.

She wasn't outside anywhere that he could see. Her boat was on the mooring, nothing in it but oars, her hens still hadn't been fed and her gumboots were on the back porch.

He pushed the back door open, not bothering to take his own boots off.

She was sitting at the table wearing her woollen cap and her coat over her nightgown, and drinking tea out of a saucer. The room smelled of wood smoke and toast.

'You spliced in razor blades!' he shouted at her.

She stopped drinking but didn't say anything.

'You put razor blades in the buoy ropes on your cray pots!'

She looked at him as though she could see right through to the bench behind him, a dead stare without a blink.

'Mum's taken him to the hospital. His hands are cut to bits!'

She turned back to her saucer and sucked her tea. 'Don't bother me with that,' she said.

'Razor blades!' he was bawling. 'All your stupid talk! Cutting down trees! Boiling crayfish! He's your brother, you crazy old looney liar! You cut his hands to bits!'

She went on drinking her tea while he went on calling her the worst names he could think of.

'How could you do that?' he yelled.

She flapped her hand at him. 'Open your eyes, boy,' she said, 'open your dopey eyes.'

# JOURNEY

The trip across Siberia is not my idea. Henry and Pru organise it as they've organised much of my life since your departure, even to buying me a set of folding coat-hangers, a sink plug and an inflatable neck pillow for the train. Henry gives me a profound talk about the benefits of travel. You remember how Henry's face and eyes actually shine when he's being profound? Well, he holds my hands between his and tells me how physical and emotional journeys coincide. He avoids words of his own like catharsis and therapeutic and instead borrows from my dictionary such expressions as transcendental and spiritual progression.

'The process from emotional death to resurrection requires movement,' Henry says.

'Besides which,' says Pru, 'you might meet someone nice. You never can tell. Stranger things have happened.'

The truth of it is they no longer want me in their house. My grief has gone on too long to be decent and they are anxious to be rid of it. I want to put my arms round them and agree that it is time I lifted my shadow from their bright buttercup rooms, but they are much too kind for the truth. Besides, getting rid of me is only the half of it. They really do believe that grief has no passport, that I'll leave it like a damp squib at Auckland airport and step on the plane, years lighter.

'You'll probably come back a raving red-head,' Henry shouts at the departure gates. 'Politically, I mean. Ha-ha-ha!'

'Have fun, Darling!' Pru insists. 'Just relax and enjoy yourself!'

Neither of them has had close acquaintance with grief or they would know that it is portable and adapts readily to different modes of travel. See, I have packed mine carefully to keep it intact, for as long as my grief is alive, so are you. In the quiet spaces I'm able to take it out, unwrap it and share with you the journey, deliberately provoking pain to prove that life is there, in me, in you, in love.

What can I tell you now? That the wilderness of Siberia is endlessly beautiful? The train rips a straight gash through dark forests of beech and fir and ice-cold rivers, through surprise meadows where people make hay in the afternoon sun. Women with white aprons and boushkas tied at the nape of the neck swing scythes in a slow wide rhythm. Men work stripped to the waist. Children run naked. Summer is hot but only six weeks long and in every village there is hay, while plots of potatoes, cabbages, onions, raspberries, grow close to the little wooden houses which look like the illustrations from old Russian fairy stories.

Yes, endlessly beautiful and endlessly full of wildflowers. Every view from the train window is splashed with yellow and blue, pink and white, the purple of willow herb and the scarlet of corn poppies. We pass at such speed that the colours run like pastels in the rain and I can barely identify the plants and butterflies among them.

I feel sorrow stir, sharp and thin-bladed. In response I reach out and embrace the memory of a man steadying a camera to capture butterflies on a buddleia bush. Do you remember that? I shook the bush for you to resettle the butterflies in a better position on the lower branches; but I shook too hard and they all flew away. You made me pose instead, a large laughing butterfly, flapping against the buddleia blossom, then, putting down your camera, you caught me and pinned me in the long summer grass.

I wish there had been time for us to say goodbye.

The small girl from the next compartment is staring at me. When I smile at her, she runs away. She is from Leningrad and is travelling back home with her mother, father, and a grandmother who has long skirts and stainless steel teeth. I think that the girl tells them that the woman next door is crying, for in a little while the old woman comes in with a smile like a new saucepan, to offer me a glass of tea and a sugar biscuit.

In the carriage there are only a few Russian travellers; the rest, I understand, are tourists from other Soviet countries. At night in the dining-car we have a party in honour of the dining-car attendant whose wife has just had a daughter. There is caviar, of course, black and salty on rye bread, with lots of vodka and red wine and more than three hours of singing. The attendant's voice is deep for a man so slight in build, and although his songs sound sentimental, the laughter they cause suggests otherwise. A group of hearty Polish men try to include me in the celebration by singing 'Waltzing Matilda'. These are the only two words they know, but they manage to repeat them in the tune with great variety of expression. 'Vossing Matilda!' they bellow. 'Vossing vossing Mati-dah!'[

When we arrive back in Irkutsk, the temperature is 36°C, the tar on the station platform sticks to our shoes like treacle and the river appears to be on fire with the sun. I didn't know Siberia could be so hot. At the hotel I stand under a cold shower for minutes, then dress and go down to the lobby to look for a postcard to send to Henry and Pru. In the shop there is also a range of books in French and English, and on impulse I buy a volume of poetry — no, not Pushkin, but an anthology of the Chinese classical poets. That's when I have the idea about the paper boat.

I've always been intrigued by the story of Li Po, how he used to write a poem on a sheet of paper which he then folded into a boat and set sail on the river. Obviously he didn't do that with all his poems. Still, it stirs my imagination that a poem should be written not for an audience but to follow its own destiny. As I think of it now, my grief forms a new energy which is cool and hard with purpose. Tomorrow I'll write for you the farewell that was never spoken, make it into a boat and take it to an ancient Siberian river which must flow forever to reach the sea.

Because it seems appropriate to ritualise every part of the action, I plan to float my farewell poem at dawn; but it isn't easy to find suitable paper. The notepaper in my pad and in the hotel is much too flimsy and I waste a couple of hours before realising that the end page of the poetry book is blank, of a good thickness and texture, and exactly right for the occasion. You, with your quick orderly mind, would have told me that at the beginning.

I miss your clear vision. It used to annoy me that you could push aside all my rainbows and go directly to the black and white heart of the matter, but now I seem to spend all my time floundering about in a rainbow maze, looking for your kind of simple answers.

In the same way I spend another two hours searching for a part of the river which looks as though it may welcome a tiny paper boat. I walk the roads of Irkutsk, with a high hot sun pressing me against the pavement and burning my enthusiasm bone-dry. Finally I find what I want, a tributary which is not small or large, neither fast nor slow, a graceful river with green banks, some rushes at the water's edge and a low stone bridge which arches over it. It is indeed beautiful, a poem in itself. I walk down to the bank and sit in the grass for a while, gathering words. Behind me there is a row of wooden houses with carved shutters shaded by apple trees. Nearby, a goat on a chain fixed to a rowan tree stands on its hind legs to nibble at some leaves. I put my bag on my knee, spread the paper over it, and write.

The words spring out with their own momentum and I am surprised at their intensity — small, simple words dragging the universe behind them. I'm about to read the poem aloud, when I hear an angry voice on the road above.

The shout is not directed at me. There are two people, a man and a woman of middle age, having a loud argument. Perhaps they are drunk. They look as though they could be. The man wears a black cap and shapeless trousers held up by both belt and braces. His voice is low and more controlled but there is fury in his body as he lurches forward at a fast pace, his hands set like claws in front of him as though he is going to pounce on someone. The woman is very large and red-faced, with thin grey hair pulled back under a scarf. She wobbles as she runs to keep up with the man, and is out of breath, but that doesn't halt the flow of words for an instant. Her voice is harsh. When she can, she jabs him in the back or on the arm with her fist.

As they reach the middle of the bridge, the man takes off his cap and throws it on the road. Then he climbs onto the stone parapet overlooking the river. The woman stops a short distance from him, and yells something that is clearly antagonistic. He yells back. He is going to jump.

I hear myself calling out, 'No! Stop!'

It almost unbalances him. He arches forward and then back, swinging his arms. The woman leans over the parapet and looks at me, shading her eyes from the sun. There is a moment of silence before she points at him and pours down on me an avalanche of thick angry words. He tries to interrupt and tell his side of the story and when she doesn't stop he shouts over her. I have become their audience. They go on and on in something like a parody of an operatic duet.

I'm aware that they don't understand my words either, but when there is a lull, I try again. 'Please! Tell him to get down from there! It's dangerous!'

The message she gives him is obviously not a warning, for he points to the water and leans forward, a gesture which she accepts with a hard laugh. She throws out her hands, offering him the whole river.

'Don't!' I cry.

The man jumps.

It happens slowly, like the replay of an Olympic dive. His hands go up, his hair rises from his forehead, his knees bend and then straighten, his boots are thrust forward. As he hits, the water comes up like a fountain, splashing over the parapet and on to the top of the bridge. Next thing, I see the man standing waist-deep in the river.

He is drenched, of course, his hair plastered down and water running over his open mouth. For a moment he just stands there, looking surprised, then he struggles to get his feet out of the mud. He looks up at the woman, who is leaning over the parapet, and a laugh comes from him, shrill, like a series of hiccups. She laughs too, snorting and shaking as she points to him, helplessly stuck in the mud. Her laughter increases as she clambers down the bank and into the rushes. Without taking off her shoes or even hitching up her skirt, she wades in, grabs his hand and pulls him out. They don't look at me. They help each other up the bank, their laughter now as loud as their anger a moment ago. She picks up his cap from the road and puts it on his head. They stagger, dripping wet and arm in arm, across the bridge, falling against each other in their new chorus.

I find that I am shivering, not with laughter but with the strange violence of it all. The water flattens, the dragonflies come back to hover over the rushes, and the goat eats the long grass round the rowan tree. But for me the flow of the river has been permanently changed and, with it, the movement of the poem. I spread the paper and read words I scarcely remember:

*Goodbye, my love,*
*I will not see you again,*
*But in the hour of my dying*
*I will breathe aloud your name.*

Did I really write that? I turn over the page and scribble:

*Knock, knock,*
*Who's there?*
*Journey.*
*Journey who?*
*Journeyed a paper boat?*

I fold the page over and over, as we used to do at school, take it to a gap in the rushes and set it afloat from the shore. It bobs like a very small pale duckling towards the stone bridge and disappears into the shadows beneath its span.

That is all.

It's a bit of an anticlimax really, with nothing of the significance promised. I walk away, irritable with the heat and thinking that if Li Po had been as humble as I'd supposed no one would know about his boat poems. But never mind, it's done now, and tomorrow I'll be back on the train, my grief all carefully packed with the coat-hangers and inflatable pillow, back among more wilderness, more memories and, with any luck, more Vossing Mati-dah.